THEY WILL KNOW

THEY WILL KNOW

BONITA FABIAN

THEY WILL KNOW

bonitafabian.com

Publishing Consultant: AuthorPreneur Publishing Inc.—
authorpreneurbooks.com
Editor: Mary Rembert—maryrembert.com
Interior Designer: Amit Dey—amitdey2528@gmail.com
Cover Designer: Zizi Iryaspraha Subiyarta

ISBN 979-8-9891674-0-1 (paperback)
ISBN 979-8-9891674-1-8 (ebook)
ISBN 979-8-9891674-2-5 (audiobook)

FIC025000 FICTION / Psychological
FIC031080 FICTION / Thrillers / Psychological

In loving memory of my parents,
Philip and Greta Badash.
And for David.

Also by Bonita Fabian

When Push Comes to Shove

CONTENTS

her and hugged her. "God put this child in our path. Accept this as a miracle."

Adela opened the cloth bag that Luca gave her. In it were a pack of diapers and an opened can of formula. The directions on the formula container were printed in a foreign language.

"What language is this?"

"Stop asking so many questions."

"What do we tell Mama?"

"Tell me what?" Signora Rosalia Melis walked into the room, buttoning up the front of her lavender house dress, her slippers slapping against the stone floor. She had just woken up from her afternoon siesta, and the back of her dark wavy hair was plastered to her scalp. She turned to see Adela feeding a baby.

"You are babysitting?" she asked, puzzled. "Is that a good idea?"

"Mama, come look. Luca found an abandoned baby. A girl."

"Excuse me?" she said, clearing her throat. "What did you say?"

"Mama," she said. "Don't talk, just listen. When Luca was away for work, he found a baby lying in the park, in the bushes, like a sign from God. She was waiting for us."

"Are you sick in the head?" Signora Melis said. "What do you mean, he brought you a baby? Luca, take this child back immediately. If you don't, I will call the police."

"Please Mama ..."

"Do you think this is the bible story where Moses was found in the bushes? What nonsense! Take her back immediately to where she came from." Signora Melis rarely raised her voice, but she was shouting.

"You know it's been hell," Luca said to his mother-in-law. "I took matters into my own hands. Adela is always telling me to be more assertive, so I am! This is a sign from God, an abandoned baby left in my path."

"You should have gone straight to the authorities," she said. "It's not a puppy, it's a child, somebody's child."

"Mama, you are always telling us about God's miracles. You are always pointing out signs and messages from God. Now that we have a sure sign, you don't accept it?" said Adela.

"Somebody didn't want her," Luca said. "I did the best thing for the baby and Adela."

"But what about this little one's parents?"

"It was probably a single mother who couldn't keep the child. So, she left her where someone would find her. This is done all the time."

"No good will come from this," Signora Melis said, putting her head in her hands. "I can't believe that we are in this predicament."

"Mama, please have a heart," pleaded Adela. "This baby will bring me peace and will heal my heart. Why must you be so negative? Luca went to a place far from here. No one will know. I am not giving this baby back."

"They will know," Signora Melis said and crossed herself.

The baby was hungry and sucked fiercely on the bottle that Adela gave her.

"We will call her Mira, *nostro miracolo*, our miracle."

When the baby stopped drinking, Adela held her against her shoulder and lightly rubbed her back until she burped.

"Ciao Mira," she said, hugging her. "Welcome to our family."

"I'm going to mass to thank God for this miracle," said Signora Melis. "Signor Rossi is returning from Napoli this evening. I will air out his room upstairs and clean up a bit."

Adela stood up with Mira in her arms and faced her mother. "Mama, Signor Rossi must never know any of this. When he left, I was pregnant, so now he will believe that this baby is the one I was expecting in the first place."

"I agree. Signor Rossi doesn't have to know that our precious Maurizio was stillborn," said Signora Melis. "When he left you were pregnant, and now that he is back, the baby is here. End of the story."

Luca sighed with relief. "It will all fall into place," he said. "Trust me; everything will work out."

Salvatore Rossi rented the upstairs apartment from Signora Melis. It was a small space: one single room with an adjoining bathroom, a compact sitting area, and a small kitchen with a table for one. Salvatore Rossi was a big man; when he stepped into his apartment, he filled the room, leaving very little space.

The apartment did not have a private entrance, so one had to enter through the Signora Melis' sky-blue wooden door and then climb the stone staircase up to the Signor Rossi's door. Due to its size and lack of privacy, the rent was not high, however, it suited both the landlady and tenant. The rent supplemented Signora Melis's monthly expenses, but she did not have to rely on it for survival. Signora Melis was left a substantial amount of money by her late husband. Therefore, Signor Rossi, a retired engineer, had a place to stay whenever he was in Oristano. He still kept his small office in Naples and would fly back and forth every few months to attend to business.

Over the years, a mutual arrangement became agreeable to both parties. Signor Rossi would oversee the maintenance of the household which included plumbing, electrical concerns, and small rodent issues.

A big part of his responsibility was the garden, which for him was more a pleasure than a chore. He tended to the Signora's small holding as if running a school for wayward children. He was firm but understanding. If the flowers did not bloom to his expectations, he covered his disappointment by treating them more gently and giving them extra attention. He even pruned the plants lovingly so that they grew faster and stronger.

But it was the fruit and vegetables that he was most proud of. The eggplants expanded like purple patent leather orbs shining in the hot sun. The bending boughs of the fig trees heavy with an abundance of ripened figs were ready to be picked before the birds took their fill. The tomatoes, the strawberries, the white asparagus, the peaches, and the plums were almost ready to be plucked by his large hands and presented in a basket to Signora Melis for inclusion in the upcoming meals.

From the beginning, Signor Rossi was a welcome guest at Signora Melis's table. He was so comfortable in the main house that he would come and go as much as he pleased. But now that Adela and Luca had moved back home, Signora Melis was concerned that the dynamics would change.

Luca and Adela had recently moved back into her mother's house soon after discovering that Adela was pregnant. Luca's truck driving job took him on the road for long stretches at a time, so it made sense for Adela to be closer to her mother.

Signora Melis and Signor Rossi had established a comfortable rhythm to their days, but with the young couple in residence, the routine was disturbed. Instead of Signor Rossi stopping in for a quick coffee in the early mornings, he now needed to make sure not to disturb the pregnant, sleeping, young woman.

"Signor Rossi is very loud in the mornings; it's disrespectful," Adela complained to her mother.

"I will tell him to be quieter," said Signora Melis.

"Why don't you tell him not to come down so early for breakfast; this is not a hotel. Besides, you know that I feel sick in the mornings and don't want to be disturbed."

"I will tell him to come down later," said Signora Melis.

Then there was the matter of the footsteps from above.

"What is the man doing up there?" said Luca. "He's like a caged animal thumping around all night."

"Signore's bedroom is right above yours; I believe he lifts weights," Signora Melis sighed.

"We took the broom and hit it hard on the ceiling to shut him up," Adela said.

Then it was a matter of the singing. Signor Rossi liked to sing in the shower. He didn't have a perfect voice, but rather it was booming and out of tune, a voice that he made up for with enthusiasm as he sang old Italian ballads. Signor Rossi brought some life back into the home, and Signora Melis would sometimes find herself humming along as she worked in the kitchen.

"If you don't tell him to shut up, I will," Adela complained. "It's the worst sound I have ever heard, like a wounded elephant trumpeting. Che facia tosta ha quest' uomo! What a nerve this man has!"

But Adela did not say anything to Signor Rossi because she knew that he was leaving soon for his five-month stay in Naples.

"Your children will be pleased that I'm going to Naples," he said the night before he left as he and Signora Melis were having dinner together.

"You know kids," she laughed, trying to make light of the situation. She usually missed having him around the house, but this time she was looking forward to less tension once he left.

The months went by slowly. Adela had a difficult pregnancy. She was nauseous most of the time. Luca worked at a large winery outside of Cagliari and delivered cases of wine by truck to towns all over Italy.

He had recently been promoted to delivering wine to neighboring countries. Although he was paid more, it was a long and arduous job that required concentration and alertness. Kilometer after kilometer, he had to sometimes force his eyes open, exhausted from the lack of sleep. He relied on his talk radio to communicate with fellow drivers, and they would talk and joke, making the hours shorter.

Most evenings, after the sun went down, Luca would turn off the road to a nearby truck stop and sleep for a few hours in his comfortable little sleeper cab on a makeshift bed. He would always call Adela to see how she was doing.

One night, when Luca was home from a long-haul trip and looking forward to a few days of rest, he came running into Signora Melis's bedroom in a panic. "Adela is bleeding!" he cried.

Signora Melis jumped out of bed and found her daughter clutching her stomach, her panties drenched with blood.

"The baby," she sobbed, hyperventilating. "I can't feel him moving."

Signora Melis helped her daughter get up off the bed and led her out the door where Luca was waiting in his idling car.

Adela was screaming from pain.

"*Stai calma*," her mother said in a quivering voice.

They arrived at the hospital and Signora Melis took Adela into the ER, where they whisked her up to the obstetrics floor. The baby, a boy, was born not breathing. He was three months too early, tiny but perfect like a dark blue rubber doll.

Signora Melis could hear her daughter's screams from down the cold, sterile hallway where she paced up and down. She felt the cold wall press behind her back as she slid down onto the linoleum floor, crouching with her head in her hands, rocking back and forth. She begged God to spare her daughter's life.

After he brought Adela home, Luca sprang into action. He shut the white cupboard doors where all the baby clothes were displayed on the shelves. He folded the baby cradle that had been sitting at the bedside and carried it down to the cellar.

Only once he was alone, between the steel shelves with the rows of jars of tomato sauce and bottles of homemade wine, did he allow himself to cry. He sat on the cold, stone floor. "Why? Why?" he sobbed, rocking back and forth. He had loved his son from the moment he was conceived. He had planned outings that they would go on together, he looked forward to teaching his son how to kick a ball, and he wanted to do all the things that his father never did with him. He was counting the days until his child was born.

"Have I sinned?" he cried out to God. "Are you punishing me?"

Luca never felt that things came easy for him. He was a slow learner at school and ridiculed for his stutter. He loved to play soccer but when trying out for the local team, season after season, he was never accepted.

It was only once he met Adela that his luck changed. He couldn't believe that she would be interested in him. She was beautiful and popular, and all the boys at school were after her, yet she chose him as her boyfriend. Adela thought he was wonderful and told him so. She laughed at his jokes and took his opinions seriously. She made him feel handsome because she thought that he was, and she was affectionate and loving. When they got married, he felt he was the luckiest man alive, and when she conceived their baby, his happiness knew no bounds. Then this happened and all his insecurities came back.

Adela lay in bed facing the wall. It was too painful for her to speak. She had imagined her whole life ahead with her baby boy. Now there would be no christening, no birthday parties, no school. A life cut short before he took his first breath.

Rosalia's only concern was for her daughter. She handled her grief by keeping busy. Making food was her way of showing love. She distracted herself by cooking and baking—her hands knew what to do even though her mind shut off. She cleaned the house with extra energy, scrubbing the marble floors on her hands and knees. She washed laundry that was still clean, wringing out the wet towels and sheets as if wrestling the devil to release her anger and frustration.

"Eat something," she begged Adela "Just a bite, just a small sip ..."

Adela turned her head away. She couldn't face her mother. She felt that she didn't deserve to eat after her baby died. Adela could barely look at Luca. She felt that she had disappointed him, that she wasn't woman enough to give him a child. Every one of her friends had healthy babies, so why not her? Did she perhaps smother him in utero by lying on her tummy? Did she not eat correctly? Was it the wine she drank before knowing that she had conceived? All these thoughts haunted her, giving her no peace or relief. Adela felt tormented at the loss of her baby, and she knew that she would never be the same again.

The more Luca tried to show her love, the more she shut him down. He wanted to scream that he was feeling lost and alone too. Everyone was concerned about Adela, but what about him?

There was only one person who Adela could find comfort with: her childhood friend, Pia Lanconi. The first thing she asked her mother was to call Pia and tell her to come right away.

Adela met Pia in grade school, and their contrasting personalities drew them to one another. Adela was shy and Pia was bold. Adela was petite for her age, while Pia was tall and robust.

At recess in the playground, Adela felt protected by her classmate. Pia's confidence perhaps was manifested as the only girl with four brothers; she learned early on to hold her own. If any of her schoolmates challenged her, her quick answers would shut them down. Adela marveled at this trait, something that she wished she had the nerve to do. She basked in her friend's safety net, and if anyone picked on her shyness or small size, Pia immediately jumped to her defense and shot them down verbally.

"You look like a baby," children would taunt her. "You shouldn't be in school. You should stay home with your mommy."

Pia, who was only seven years old, would march up to the offender, stand tall, puff her chest out, and say, "Say that again to my face and your mama will have to come get you at the hospital."

Even the teachers were wary of her.

"I don't want this old, used book," Pia said to her second-grade teacher. "I want a new book."

"Take your seat," said the teacher. "We will discuss the books after we have settled down."

Although Pia didn't get a new book, the teacher noted that she was a challenge.

"I don't want to sit so close to the board," grumbled Pia. "I like to sit in the back."

"Pia Lanconi, you will sit where I tell you to sit," said the teacher, pursing her lips.

"I don't think so," said Pia, getting out of her seat and striding toward Adela in the back row. She edged herself onto the chair so that Adela had to move up and make a place for her, and when the teacher told Pia to see her after class, Adela understood that this girl was the one she needed on her side.

They did not end up sharing a desk, but they did sit alongside each other for the rest of the school year. Throughout the school years, the summers, and the trials and tribulations of their teenage years, Adela Messi and Pia Lanconi were inseparable. Pia, the daring blonde, egged on Adela, the small brunette, to smoke, to drink, to skip days from school, and the toughest of all, to not care what other people thought.

So, it made sense why Pia was the first person that Adela wanted to comfort her after she lost the baby. Pia knew how much this baby meant to her. Ever since she was a young girl, Adela's future dream was to be a mother. When Adela married Luca, Pia was happy for her, but she understood the laws of friendship and love; now she would play second fiddle to Luca. Even though the girls had sworn eternal loyalty to one another, when Luca came home from work, Adela had to be there for him.

Pia had her share of getting her heart broken; she had been burned many times by the wrong choice of partners. She was attracted to bad boys, and those boys treated her badly.

"Find someone as caring as Luca," Adela told her. "Someone hardworking and stable who puts his family first."

Pia was sixteen when the color of her life turned gray. Her mother had ignored a black smudge on her shoulder and later found out at the hospital that she had melanoma, a deadly cancer that had already spread to her lungs. She died before Pia and her father could process the shock. Her father, a simple olive tree farmer, could not cope with his loss and started dating younger women as soon as his wife was buried. Her older brothers took different paths with their grief and Pia soon found out that they didn't have her well-being in mind.

Pia gravitated toward Adela and her mother. They took her into their fold, with no words, just acceptance. She moved into their home, with a bedroom of her own. Pia fitted in like a second daughter. Signora Melis enjoyed the liveliness and happy spirit that she brought into their home. Pia helped in the kitchen and kept the house tidy; she also knew when to be unobtrusive and stay in her room. Adela and Pia were like sisters. They had a natural sibling rivalry where they bitched and complained with one another, but their close bond was hard to break. After high school, Pia moved out of the house to a nearby village where she had a job as an apprentice hairdresser.

It was Pia who Adela wanted in her time of loss. Luca, suffering from his pain, welcomed Pia's support. She rushed over immediately and sat at Adela's bedside, and held her hand without saying a word.

"They took out my uterus," cried Adela. "There were complications."

"What does that mean?" asked Pia quietly.

"It means that I can never have another baby."

As Adela wept, Pia wiped her tears and brushed her hair away from her wet face. For the next few days, Pia came every day to sit with her friend.

Sometimes Luca joined them, and they reminisced about their teenage days and even made Adela laugh at some of their silly antics.

One morning, just like that, Adela got out of bed, took a shower, washed her hair, got dressed, and asked Luca to walk with her to town to eat at Mama Sofia's Trattoria.

"We have such good things to eat at home," said Signora Melis. "I can make all your favorite food."

"No one cooks like you, Mama," said Adela. "But I need to go out and join the living again."

CHAPTER THREE

DENMARK

Looking through the window was like a snow globe that had just been shaken. Light snow was falling, and seated inside the living room, facing a roaring fire, were Jens and Gudrun Nielsen. On the adjacent sofa sat their daughter Astrid, her husband Anton, and their newborn baby girl, Anja. Nanna, seated in a rocker close by, was nodding off, lulled by the heavy Christmas meal and the warmth of the fire.

"Christmas couldn't be any more joyful than with the addition of little Anja," said Gudrun, tucking a piece of stray hair into her bun. "Our prayers were answered."

Everyone agreed by raising their glasses of glogg, a mulled wine. "*God Jul!*—Merry Christmas!" they cried "To Anja's first Christmas. *Skol!*"

A rotund fresh fir tree, anchored in the center of the room, was decorated with the Danish colors of white and red. Twinkling white fairy lights were strung around its girth like a festive hula dancer, with candles flickering brightly between the branches.

Jens let out a big yawn and said, "Well done ladies. The dinner was a great success."

"And you too, Jens," Gudrun said. "You helped so much by setting everything up and making the room look festive. The roast duck, potatoes, and vegetables were delicious. Unfortunately, the cherry sauce on my risalamande was too sweet."

"It was perfect," they all agreed. "As good as always."

Gudrun had a habit of downplaying her culinary efforts—always too sweet, not sweet enough, too dry, a total flop, whereas it was always just right. It was her greatest fear to disappoint her dinner guests.

"OK, everyone stand up! It's time to dance around the tree," said Jens. "Don't be lazy."

They all eagerly jumped up, forming a circle around the tree and reaching for each other's hands. They started singing, "Now It's Christmas Again." Slowly they circled the tree, picking up the pace, until they were almost at a jog. They giggled as they sang, loudly and out of tune. After a few rounds, they turned in the other direction, starting all over again. Soon they were all out of breath and the circle fell apart.

Anja, who was now awake and suckling at Astrid's breast, was oblivious to all the fun. Anton bent down, kissed his baby daughter on her head, and said, "Next year, you will be dancing with us."

"Traditions are a wonderful thing," said Gudrun. "I remember Astrid as a toddler dancing around the tree, and now her daughter will be dancing soon."

For the first two weeks of Anja's life, Anton and Astrid were given time off from their work to bond with their new baby. Thereafter, they had fifty-two weeks divided between the two of them to spend time adjusting and raising their daughter. Anton was a high school math teacher and Astrid was a graphic designer for an online toy manufacturer. They both had decided that Astrid would take the first six months to stay home with Anja and Anton would take off the following six months. They were both on paid leave so they didn't have to worry about loss of income.

"OK guys, I am off to bed," said Jens. "*Godnat*, sleep well."

Astrid went upstairs with the baby while Anton stayed behind to help his mother-in-law clean up.

"I am so happy to see Astrid coping so well with the baby," Gudrun said, wiping down the kitchen counters with a cloth. "It was a tough pregnancy for both of you, especially the last month."

"Oh yes indeed," Anton replied. "With Astrid's high blood pressure, we didn't know if the pregnancy would go full-term, but luckily Anja came only two weeks early."

"It was a long and stressful journey to conceive," said Gudrun. "All the treatments, the injections, the hormones—followed by the disappointments. Then just like that, when you had both decided you couldn't take it anymore, a miracle happened. Our baby was conceived!"

"*Ja*," Anton said. "We are so fortunate. A healthy baby, what more could we ask for?"

After everything was put away, Gudrun quietly woke her mother up from a deep sleep and helped her to bed. She could hear Astrid singing softly to Anja.

"Life is good," she said to herself.

In the morning, after coffee, rye bread with cheese, and soft-boiled eggs, the family gathered in the same places as the night before. Gudrun lit the fire, and they all agreed to put away their phones and read until it was time for the next meal. "Let's be *hygge*," they said. "Just cozy, lazy, and content being with the ones we love."

That is how they spent the rest of Christmas day. They ate, drank, talked, and napped. Life was good in Denmark; they didn't know that everything was about to change. Maybe that was for the best, maybe it wasn't.

It had snowed the whole night and the family woke up to white powder covering half of the windows and compacted against the front and back door.

Jens, bundled up in a warm coat, a woolen cap, gloves, and rubber boots had already shoveled the path to the kitchen door.

"I spoke to Harald early this morning. He said we must still come over for lunch," Jens said to his wife.

"Oh stop," laughed Astrid. "I saw your baby pictures and you were so cute."

"She looks like every newborn baby," said Aksel. "Ugly."

They moved to the large, round wooden table that was set with colorful placemats and red pottery plates. Clara placed a big ceramic bowl in the center of the table with steaming meatballs in a rich creamy sauce, along with a platter of boiled potatoes with parsley and butter. She always served her homemade pickled cucumber salad with every meal.

"Help yourselves," said Clara, wiping the sweat off her brow with the corner of her apron, her face flushed from the heat of the stove.

The room became silent as each person tucked into their meal. The only sound was their chewing and swallowing, ending with a huge burp from Jens.

"Forgive me," he said.

"In some cultures, that's a sign of appreciation of the meal," laughed Gudrun.

"In Danish culture, that's a sign of rudeness," said Aksel.

"Ah well, anyone have an interesting story to tell?" said Dr. Sorensen.

"I do," said Astrid.

"So do I," said Gudrun.

"Astrid, you go first," said Dr. Sorensen.

"You know the Johansen family on the corner? They have a university exchange student from America staying with them."

"Ja, I've seen her at the supermarket, a pretty girl," said Clara.

"I don't like to gossip, but guess what? Pastor Johansen, from our church, is having an affair with her."

Everyone stopped eating and looked up in shock.

"You don't say!" said Clara, shaking her head.

"I was with Pastor Johansen's daughter, Lara, at the park a few days ago," continued Astrid. "We both took the babies out for some fresh air, and she told me."

"My goodness," said Jens. "She must have been very upset."

"Actually, she was quite matter-of-fact. She said that her mother has agreed to let the girl stay on in the house."

"Wow, that's a modern concept," said Anton.

"Things are certainly different these days," said Gudrun. She turned to Clara. "What's your story, Clara?"

"My story is so boring compared to that," she said. "I was going to tell you all that we found an outside cat and that we are keeping it but that sounds so trivial now."

"Not so different," laughed Jens. "You found a new pussy and Pastor Erik Johansen found a new pussy too."

"Father!" said Astrid, shocked. She had never heard him be vulgar before.

They all laughed hard except for Clara; she looked down at her crocheting, pursing her lips in disapproval.

window facing their strollers. Astrid gasped and pressed her head to the glass window. "Oh my God," she shouted, running toward the door.

"What's wrong?" said Lara, following her friend's gaze.

"Where is my baby?" Astrid screamed.

The stroller was pushed slightly against the wall and the top blanket pulled over to the side. There was an oval indent where the baby had lain. Anja was gone.

Lara raced out the door behind Astrid. When she saw that Oliver was still asleep in his stroller, she gasped from relief.

"Where's Anja?" she said in panic while picking up Oliver and clutching him to her chest.

"My baby!" wailed Astrid. "Help! Help me!" she screamed. She frantically pulled back the covers to see if Anja was buried beneath—she was not.

People started gathering, silently, in shock—one older woman put her arms around Astrid, attempting to calm her, but Astrid tore herself away.

"Call the police!" someone yelled, while others sprang into action, running in all directions looking for someone carrying a baby.

"It could be a mistake," said the Café owner. "Who would take a baby?"

No stranger had ever taken a child from a parked stroller before, so no one could grasp how this could happen.

The police arrived in two cars with sirens blaring. They found Astrid on her knees in the street, screaming hysterically.

They screened off the area and took precautions not to disturb the crime scene. No one had ever taken a baby in that town before. It was customary for parents to leave their sleeping babies outside restaurants or stores.

Like most parents, Astrid had a baby monitor attached to the top of the stroller that was connected to her cell phone. That was the first thing the police checked, but the monitor had not been activated on that day.

"I want my mother," Astrid sobbed in Lara's arms. "Get my Mama."

"Anton is on his way," Lara said.

"What am I going to say to my husband?" Astrid cried. "It's my fault. I wasn't paying attention. Now my baby is gone."

Anton arrived, pale and distraught. He held Astrid in his arms. "It could be a mistake," he said. "Someone took her by mistake."

Police helicopters were flying above, police with sniffer dogs were scouring the area, and the media had arrived with television cameras and photographers.

Gudrun and Jens arrived and helped Astrid into the car, where she sat slumped and silent. There were no more tears, only an icy cold feeling spread through her body.

"Is this a bad dream?" she asked her mother as she rocked her.

A female detective approached Astrid and asked her to go over every detail. She was too panicked to think.

"I don't know. I can't remember anything," she said, then thrust open the car door and threw up onto the street.

After breakfast, Signora Melis, Signor Rossi, Adela, and Luca, pushing Mira in the stroller, walked the few blocks to Piazza Manoa. Pia joined them halfway. It was a beautiful, warm day with a cool breeze. The drumming added to the thrill of anticipation. The whole town had come out for the racing event.

Their seats up front in the stands gave them a perfect view. Mira, startled by the loud drumming, started crying. Pia took her from Luca's arms and gently rocked her. Mira immediately stopped crying, put her head on Pia's shoulder, and closed her eyes.

"She adores you," said Adela, smiling.

The riders, dressed in traditional Oristano costumes, lined up on their horses. The goal was to try and catch a star-shaped ring with their swords, and the team with the most stars wins the race.

Pia spotted Alessandro in the line on his horse. She nudged Adela. When the race started, she was aware of how many young girls were rooting for him by calling out his name.

The red and blue teams left the piazza on their horses and raced down the streets toward the Piazza Duomo. As soon as they left, the family left the stands and found a table and chairs under a large shady tree. Enclosures were set up with food for the carnival. Large pots of steaming meatballs, homemade pasta, pizza slices, chicken simmering in a tomato sauce, and an array of paninis were part of the feast.

"Your food is good?" Signora Melis asked Signor Rossi.

"I'm eating well," he said. "Of course, not as good as your cooking."

Signora Melis smiled broadly. Nothing made her happier than people enjoying her cooking. She showed her love through her food, and everyone felt it.

After a few beers, Salvatore Rossi was in a jovial mood. He sang along with the live band, wrapping his large arms around Luca's shoulders, swaying back and forth. Adela held Mira up on her lap, swinging her gently to the music.

After a while, Luca, distracted by the soccer scores on his phone, paid little attention to the surroundings.

"Luca, come on," said Adela. "You are missing out on all the fun."

"It's my one day to relax," he said. "Tomorrow I'm on the road again."

"Aw poor baby," mocked Pia. "You have such a hard life."

She leaned over and passed Mira over to him. "Take your baby," she said. "Give your wife a break."

Just then Claudia, pushing a stroller with her baby, walked over. "*Ciao*, having a good time?" she asked.

"Of course," said Adela.

"Giorgio says 'ciao' to everybody. He is working today; doctors don't get a break," she said. "*Mamma mia*! Mira is so tiny; our babies were born at the same time but he is twice her size."

"Girls are generally smaller," said Signora Melis, annoyed.

"Who is your pediatrician?" Claudia asked.

"Did your friend Lara tell anyone where she was going?" he asked.

"She only told her husband," Astrid said.

"Did you see anyone outside by the strollers?"

"No."

"Were there people outside at that time?"

"I didn't notice," Astrid said; tearing up. Anton reached for her hand.

"Do you have a baby monitor on your baby carriage?"

"Yes," Astrid said in a whisper. She clenched her fists and looked down. "But I didn't turn it on."

"Why?"

"I forgot." Astrid rocked back and forth crying.

"Does your friend have a baby monitor?"

"I don't know."

Detective Borgen turned to Anton. "Where were you on the day that Astrid went for a walk?"

"I was at the high school where I teach," he said. The detective took down the name of the school to verify the information.

"Are you currently working?" he asked Astrid.

"No, I am taking care of the baby for the first six months and then will switch with my husband," she said. "I was taking care of the baby. Oh my God, I was supposed to be taking care of her, and look what happened?" she cried.

"Tissues please," he called out to Clara. She returned with a box of tissues and the detective passed one to Astrid.

"There is one other thing I just remembered," Astrid said to the detective.

"Yes?" he said.

"The volume of the TV in the restaurant was on very loud, so we couldn't hear ourselves speak. I asked the waitress to turn down the sound, and she did. I think that's when I was distracted and didn't check the stroller."

"We can find out the time that happened," said Detective Borgen. "That might give us an idea of a timeline."

He then turned to Clara. "Excuse me *Frue*," he said. "Who lives in this house?"

"My husband, me, and our son, Aksel."

"Please write down your full names and ages," he said to Clara. "And give the information to Detective Olsen."

He then asked Astrid where she, Anton, and Anja lived. She gave him the address of their house, which was not far from her parents' house.

"Since Anja was born, we have spent a lot of nights at my parents' house. Their house is next door to this one. I was raised in that house and our neighbors, the Sorensens, are like family to us."

"We are so distraught," said Clara. "Astrid is like a daughter to us, and Anja is like a granddaughter." With tears in her eyes, she blew her nose.

The detective continued his questioning. "Does anyone else besides your parents live at their home?"

"My grandmother," Astrid said. "She has Alzheimer's."

The detective nodded his head and bit his bottom lip. "Mrs. Larsen," he said, looking at Astrid very closely, "Do you know of anyone that would want to take the baby? Is anyone jealous of you? Perhaps someone who wants a baby? Have you noticed anyone paying special attention to the baby?"

Astrid thought for a minute. "No. No one at all," she said. "Everyone was happy for us."

Detective Borgen addressed the same questions to Anton. He also could not think of anyone who would want to steal their child. "How long does it take to find a missing child?" Astrid interjected.

The detective shot a glance at his colleague. "We will do everything we can to find her," he said. "In the meantime, if you have any ideas or questions, call me at once." He handed them a card with his contact information.

"But what is the average timeframe for finding a kidnapped child?" she asked again.

"We don't have a long history of this. We don't know," Detective Olsen said.

"I once read that if you don't find the victim within forty-eight hours, the chances become slimmer. Is that true?" asked Anton.

"Each case is different," said the detective. "There is no set formula. We will do our utmost best to get the baby back to you as soon as possible."

After they left, Astrid asked Anton to take her next door to her mother. As soon as she opened the door, she fell onto the sofa, crying. Gudrun jumped up and closed Anja's nursery door.

"Mother, don't do that," she said. "I want her door open. I can still feel her in there; I can still smell her baby smell."

Gudrun reopened the door.

"We have to believe that Anja will come back. We have to carry on with hope. Keep her nursery door open so we can see her clothes hanging in her closet waiting for her. I have to believe that she will be back soon, otherwise I might as well just end it right now."

"Yes," said her mother. "We will not give up hope."

Jens added, "We have hope, and we will pray for her return as fast as possible."

"We will be strong," said Anton. "We are strong people, and we don't give up."

Nanna sat in her recliner for most of the day, only getting up to eat or go to the bathroom. They had placed her chair facing the window so that she could look out at the garden, the street, and the neighbors walking by. Her mind meandered back to her childhood, and she spoke of her parents as if they were still there. Now and again the fog would clear, and she would say something astute that surprised the family.

"Where is the baby?" she asked out loud.

Gudrun swiveled her head toward her mother. "She was taken away," she said. "We are very sad. We don't know where she is."

"She will come back," the old lady said, her voice strong, while picking food out of her tooth with her fingernail. "She is in a safe place by the water."

"The water?" said Astrid. "Why would you say that Nanna?"

The old lady yawned, closed her eyes, and went to sleep.

CHAPTER EIGHT

SARDINIA

The church bells rang for the early morning mass. Signora Melis washed her face, combed her hair, and put on one of her many floral summer dresses. She didn't find it necessary to put on makeup and preferred her face natural. Just as God intended, she explained. Adela begged her mother to put on a bit of lipstick, some mascara, and blush.

"Mama, you could look so pretty," she said. "You have a lovely face; you should bring out your features more."

"I'm fine just the way I am," said Signora Melis. She had been over this so many times with her daughter that she was becoming annoyed. "Why? Don't you think I look good?"

"You look fine, mama. But you could look better, that's all that I'm saying."

"I don't want to waste my time on such nonsense," said Signora Melis. "Everyone has to accept me the way I am."

"You should at least put on moisturizer," said Adela. "The sun is not good for any of our skin."

"It's too late," said Signora Melis. "My skin already looks like a pressed flower. When I was a child, I used to pick flowers and place them between tissue paper in the center of my big bible. After a few weeks, they had dried transparent and fragile. That's how my skin looks," she laughed.

Signora Melis didn't even check herself in the mirror before she left the house to walk the fifty steps to the corner cathedral. She could have walked there in her sleep; she knew the path so well.

Mass had been a part of her everyday life for so many years that it was akin to breathing, eating, and sleeping. She had gone twice a day ever since her late husband Matteo was diagnosed with liver cancer ten years ago. Despite the harsh medical treatments, chemotherapy and radiation, he died a few months after his diagnosis. By the time he went to the doctor, the cancer had already spread to his brain. Signora Melis had prayed so diligently for the Lord to heal him, but when he succumbed to the disease, she accepted that as God's will, and she was not bitter. She felt a deep comfort in the cathedral and continued her faith by attending daily mass.

Signora Melis missed her husband; he was a man who took charge. His philosophy was that there are no problems, only solutions. Signora Melis worried about everything, so she admired his "can do" attitude and wished she could be more like him. If something needed to change, he jumped into action, whereas anxiety would paralyze her unless she was in the kitchen cooking. Now that he was gone, she missed his strengths and being able to rely on him. But she also discovered something else that she did not know before. She liked her newfound independence and not having to answer to him. She realized for the first time in her life that she was very capable of making the right decisions and that she had inner strengths that she didn't know of before. As the years went by, Signora Melis developed a confidence that even surprised her. She walked straighter, had a bounce in her step, and could look people in the eye and give her opinion.

She went from being an obedient well-behaved daughter, never questioning her parents' decisions, to an obedient hardworking wife of a husband who ruled the house as an antiquated chauvinist. She was now an independent woman with an independent mind. Even though she wouldn't admit it, Signora Melis was a happier woman since her husband had died.

Signor Melis had owned a Tabacchi store just off the Piazza Eleanora, a convenience store where you could buy anything and everything—cigarettes, stamps, snacks, pay your bills, mail your postcards, and buy lotto tickets, bus tickets, and phone cards. It was also a gathering place for his friends to meet up in the small back room to have an espresso while debating the pros and cons of the local soccer team. The Tabacchi was open after everything else was closed, so if you forgot to buy anything, you could still get it there on your way home. Matteo's male friends hung out there to keep him company. They enjoyed arguing and laughing about political policies and general affairs in Italy. They had an opinion about everything and everyone. On warm summer evenings, the men congregated outside, sitting at the tables on the sidewalk with an Aperol spritz in one hand and a cigar in the other. They patiently waited for Matteo to clean and lock up, procrastinating about going home to their wives and family.

Signora Melis was a good wife. She cooked tasty meals and saw to her husband's laundry and ironing. She kept the house spotless. Apart from conversations about everyday things, they rarely spoke to each other. They would discuss things to do with Adela, her school, her homework, or more importantly, what Signora Melis was going to prepare that night for dinner. She had her pulse on the gossip in town, but Matteo had no interest in that. He did not enjoy small talk, he told her that often. She reminded him that the conversations he enjoyed with his friends were not about brain surgery either. They had a traditional marriage. He was the breadwinner, and she handled everything to do with running the household.

When Matteo died, his true nature was revealed. Although he had a tough exterior, he had a kind heart. He left everything that he owned to his wife, Signora Melis—the house, the car, his gold watch and jewelry, and the Tabacchi. When the mourning period was over, Signora

Melis sold the Tabacchi for a substantial sum, which allowed her to live a comfortable life, not lacking for anything.

Signora Melis pushed open the heavy doors and immediately felt the cool air brush against her cheeks. She loved the smell of the church, the leather, the books, the wood, and the burning candles. If she could bottle it and wear it as her perfume she would. Eau de Basilica, she would call it.

Signora Melis approached the darkened vestibule, lit by rows of candles casting dancing shadows on the stone walls like an old black-and-white movie. A marble statue of the Madonna tenderly cradling her baby son filled her soul with joy. She lit a candle for her husband and her mother. She could have included her mother-in-law, but Signora Melis never liked the woman in life, so she wasn't concerned about her soul in death. She crossed herself and knelt.

When she finished her prayers, Padre Selvio floated toward her like an apparition in a long black robe. Signora Melis had known him for many years, and even though they may have been similar ages, she always regarded him as an elderly, wise sage.

"*Bongiorno Padre*," she greeted him.

He smiled, holding his arms out toward her, enveloping her in his warmth without touching.

"I missed you yesterday, Signora," he said, smiling.

"Yes, we went to Su Saratiglia." Then she added, "I said my rosary before I left."

"God hears your prayers from wherever you are," the Padre answered. "Everything good with you today?" he asked.

The word "yes" stuck in her throat. She coughed nervously. Senora Melis wanted to tell him everything, to confess about the baby, but she knew that she could not. Even if he believed in miracles, would he believe that Mira was a miracle? She had to force herself to keep quiet, smiling instead. She wished him a blessed day as she left.

Luca and Adela sat in the piazza, eating ice cream. Mira, very contently sitting in her stroller, was making baby sounds.

"She is so cute, I could eat her up," said Adela, gazing at her baby lovingly.

"Me too," said Luca. "She is a happy baby. We are fortunate she has a sweet nature."

Adela took a bite of her Stracciatella ice cream, licking the edges of the cone so it wouldn't drip. "I feel so bad," she suddenly said, seriously. "When I think about it, I can't believe what we did."

"*Amore*, don't think about it," he said. "Remember what we promised? We have to be strong for Mira. God put her in our path for a reason."

Adela leaned in and whispered, "Can you tell me just one thing? Where was she born?"

"No good would come of it if you knew. Trust me on this," he answered tensely.

"Was it another country? I feel if you told me more this would be easier for me. There are so many unanswered questions. The mystery makes it hard, don't you understand that?" she said. "I know that she was loved and well cared for because she was found clean and well dressed."

Luca licked his ice cream and was silent. He couldn't look his wife in the face, and he felt terrible about it.

"One day I will tell you more," he said. "I know that you don't understand now, but the less you know, the easier this will be."

"I don't know why you think that?" Adela said. "Surely the more I know, the better it will be for all of us."

"Please Adela, just trust me. I love you and I want you to be happy. That is all I want."

"All I do know is that we love her with all our heart and soul and will protect her forever," Adela said, looking at her child.

"That's all we have to know," Luca said. "There *is* one thing that we need to discuss."

Adela turned to face him.

"We need to get Mira a birth certificate. I have to decide how to go about it. I have some ideas," Luca said.

"Is that a problem?" she asked. "How can she get a birth certificate, when we don't know any details? It will be impossible."

"I happen to know someone who can forge a birth certificate, but it will cost a lot of money."

"That sounds like a bad idea," Adela said.

"We don't have an option."

Who is this person?" Adela said as she bit her nail. "Isn't it illegal?"

Luca leaned in, one leg bouncing up and down under the table. He hesitated, then whispered, "Alessandro."

"Alessandro? Pia's Alessandro!" she exclaimed. "No way! Are you sure?"

"*Si.* I told you that he is a piece of shit and does shady stuff."

"Does Pia know?" she said.

"She is the one who told me about him. That's how he makes his money." Luca ran his hand nervously through his hair. "Pia is the only one who knows the truth about Mira. You know that. Therefore, she is the only person we can trust."

"How much will it cost?" Adela asked.

"I'll ask him," Luca said. "He knows when people are desperate, he can name his price."

"I wish it wasn't him. He is the worst person to involve in this," Adela said.

'I agree, but it's people like him who do illegal things and we need him."

They walked back home in silence; a bolt of lightning lit up the dark sky, followed by the rumble of thunder. Mira, oblivious to the upcoming storm, slept peacefully.

They came home to a commotion. Signora Melis was standing in knee-deep water, wringing out towels into a big bucket. Signor Rossi, his pants hitched up to his knees, was also twisting wet towels into the bucket. They worked as a team, fast and furious, while water swished back and forth between their legs. The entire lower level of the house was flooded.

"*Dio Mio*!" cried Adela. "What happened?"

"A pipe burst in the Signora's bathroom," said Signor Rossi. "We were about to sit down to dinner when I heard the sound of rushing water. I immediately jumped up, found the source, and turned off the main valve, but the water was so powerful that there is a lot of damage."

Luca and Adela walked barefoot through the house. All the rooms, including their bedroom, were underwater. The furniture and the rugs were piled up on the beds. The place was a mess.

"I need to mop up your bedroom next," said Signor Rossi to Adela. "The baby has to have her area organized so that she can go to sleep. I will try my best to make it dry."

"How can I help?" said Luca.

"You can finish drying the kitchen floor, your mother is working on the living room, and I will get your room ready for Mira," Signor Rossi said, taking charge. "Adela, you take the baby upstairs to my place and keep her away from the disaster."

Adela took Signor Rossi's advice and walked up the stairs with Mira. The three others worked in tandem, mopping up the floors. Then Signor Rossi took the large squeegee into the young family's bedroom. Methodically, he pulled and pushed, then squeezed the water into the bucket. When the water on the stone floor was almost dry, he wiped the sweat off his brow with his sleeve and proceeded to rearrange the bedroom furniture. He pushed Mira's crib into place, packed away the clothes lying on the bed, and put random papers back in the drawers.

A few hours later, it looked like nothing had ever happened, the house looked like it had just been spring-cleaned.

"*Grazie mille Salvatore*, thanks a thousand times," said Signora Melis. "I don't know what we would have done without you."

"Yes," said Adela. "You saved the day."

After a simple dinner, the family went to bed earlier than usual. Everyone was exhausted. Signor Rossi went up the stairs and sat on his bed. He was tired, but first, he needed to do something. He made sure that his bedroom door was shut. It didn't have a lock, so he moved his desk against the door so that no one could get in.

He took out a folded newspaper cutting from his pocket, spread it out on his bed, and turned the table lamp on to illuminate the page.

The newspaper was written in a foreign language, one that he did not recognize. The headlines were in bold black ink and even though he couldn't understand all the words, he got the message. He gasped.

There was a photograph of a young couple with stricken expressions standing next to uniformed officers. In a separate black-and-white photo was the image of a small baby. What he understood immediately was that the baby was missing, and they were asking for the public's help.

He looked at the date of the newspaper. It was dated three months earlier.

Signor Rossi's chest tightened, and he couldn't breathe. He stood up and paced the floor. Why was this newspaper cutting hidden in Luca's bedside drawer? A puzzle started forming in Salvatore Rossi's mind—he was previously told that Adela was having a boy before he left for Naples, so when he returned, he had been surprised that the baby was a girl. Mira's age didn't add up; she was younger than she should have been. She was fair, blue-eyed, and blonde, and her parents had dark hair, dark eyes, and olive skin.

He argued with himself. *You are just crazy*, he thought. What language was this? He looked at the page and saw that the city was Copenhagen. Denmark? How does this tie into Adela and Luca? Signor Rossi was stunned. s tired as he was, his mind raced all night. He knew that he had to get to the bottom of this.

CHAPTER NINE

DENMARK

Astrid's days became weirdly structured, there was a routine to loss and grieving. The day always started with hope—maybe this was the day that Anja would be found. By the time midday came around and the family had been updated by the police, hopelessness took over. It was the nights that were the worst. Darkness and desperation do not mix well. Questions without answers haunted Astrid. What if Anja was suffering? What if she wasn't taken care of? And usually, just before dawn, the worst feeling of doom overcame Astrid, what if Anja was dead?

Sometimes Astrid would dream that everything was like before. She was rocking her baby in her arms, feeding her at her breast, marveling at her perfection. Then she would awaken to her reality of a nightmare.

Anton and Astrid were becoming strangers. They both functioned but in parallel dimensions, although at times they clung to one another in desperation, as if they were the only two people suffering the same devastation, the loss of their child.

Although he never said it, Astrid felt that deep down Anton was blaming her.

How could she have not been aware that Anja was stolen? Why was she not paying more attention? Babies are left sleeping outside alone all the time but none have gone missing. She beat herself up as to why the monitor wasn't turned on. Why hadn't she looked out the window to check on Anja at that time? Why was she distracted by the loud TV? She blamed and hated herself.

"Where are you going?" said her mother. Astrid had her coat on and was walking out the door.

"I'm going to get some fresh air," she said, resenting her mother for watching every move she made.

"Don't go too far," said Gudrun.

Astrid walked briskly to the park. On the way there, she saw flyers posted in shop windows with photos of her missing baby. The beautiful, innocent face of her missing daughter was like a punch to her soul. She passed pink ribbons tied to the trunks of trees as a sign of hope for Anja's return. It seemed like the whole town was searching for her baby, yet there was someone out there who took her. She entered the park like a zombie, feeling numb. This was the last place that she was with Anja, when she was happy and oblivious to the terrible event that was to come.

She had spoken to Lara, but she was not ready to see her in person. Astrid felt no ill will that Lara's son Oliver was safe, but she couldn't reconcile that her baby was the one taken that day. Was it random or was she targeted? She went over and over every person that she knew, trying to recall every person that she had met in passing, looking for clues to remember anyone who had acted suspiciously.

Astrid sat on the same bench that they had sat on, trying to jog her memory about every detail of that day. The ducks were still swimming in the lake, but now there were no ducklings. She wondered what happened to those ducklings who trailed their mother in circles the last time that she was there.

Astrid was deep in thought when she heard soft crying. She looked up and on the bench alongside her, a girl was wiping her tears with a crumpled tissue. She sniffed, then stopped and blew her nose, then sniffed again, wiping her tears with her finger. She was a pretty girl in her early twenties, petite and blonde, wearing a gray sweatsuit and Nike sneakers. When Astrid glanced at her, she stopped crying and started scrolling on her cell phone as if she was reading something important.

"*Har du det godt*?" said Astrid.

"Sorry, I don't speak Danish," the girl said in an American accent.

"Are you OK?" Astrid repeated in English.

"Not really, but I'm trying to be," she answered, smiling wanly.

"Where are you from?" said Astrid.

"I'm American, and I'm here as an exchange student."

"Do you live in the neighborhood?" asked Astrid, wondering if this could be who she thought it was.

"Yes, I was staying with the Johansen family. Erik and Anna Johansen."

"Oh, I know them well." Astrid moved closer to her. "I heard that they had an exchange student from America. I'm friendly with their daughter Lara."

"Oh, please don't tell them that you saw me crying," she said, rubbing her tears away.

"I won't," said Astrid. "I'm sorry that you are crying."

"I'm just mad at myself for ruining things," the girl said. "I'm Carly."

"I'm Astrid. Astrid Larsen," she said. "I'm going through my own sadness. My baby was taken three weeks ago; we can't find her."

Astrid immediately put her hand over her mouth, surprised that she had blurted that out.

The girl got up from the bench and walked toward her.

"I'm so sorry," she said. "I heard all about it. You must be devastated." She looked at Astrid with concern. Astrid felt the sincerity in her voice, and it touched her.

Carly sat down beside her. "I can't imagine anything worse."

"I know," said Astrid, with tears in her eyes.

"I am aware that the community is very worried and concerned about the baby," Carly said. "Everyone is trying to find her. I know there is not much I can do, but I will pray that she will come home soon."

"Why were you crying?" asked Astrid.

"I have a problem. It's trivial compared to yours. Pastor and Mrs. Johansen just told me that I have to leave, and I have nowhere to go."

"Has your college year ended?" Astrid asked. She knew that this was the girl who was having an affair with Lara's father.

"It ended some time back, and the couple let me stay on. They have now changed their minds," she said.

"They must have a reason, don't you think?" said Astrid.

"They do; I get it." Carly looked down and flicked invisible crumbs from her lap. "This sounds bad, but I was having a relationship with the pastor. His wife found out, and of course, it's not good."

"It never is good," said Astrid.

"The leaders of the Lutheran church found out. They told the pastor that either he ends it with me, or he has to leave. They said that this situation is not consistent with the teachings of the church."

"That makes sense," said Astrid. "Where are you going to go?"

"I will go back to my hometown in the States. In the meantime, I will look for a place on Snaregade."

"It's not for me to judge, but I feel sorry for Mrs. Johansen," said Astrid.

"Everyone hates me, but Erik is half to blame too. There were two of us in the relationship." Carly blew her nose one last time and threw the crumpled tissue into a nearby bin.

When Astrid had heard about the affair, she had imagined a brazen femme fatale ruthlessly chasing the pastor. Now she saw a young, scared, vulnerable girl who looked lost, and her heart softened a little. Pastor Johansen had been rumored to have had a few flings in his time, so Carly probably wasn't the first nor would she be the last, thought Astrid.

They both stood up and shook hands awkwardly like strangers, even though they had just shared personal information. They waved goodbye and walked home in opposite directions.

Astrid came home to find her mother picking Nanna up from the floor.

"She fell flat on her face," Gudrun said. "Help me get her to the couch."

Astrid put her arm around Nanna's shoulder and slowly walked her to the sofa.

"Where does it hurt?" Gudrun asked her mother.

"Where does it hurt?" said the old lady, rubbing her leg as she lay down.

"Your leg?" asked Gudrun, placing her hand on her mother's leg. "Here?" she asked, placing her hand on her hip.

"Stop this nonsense!" said Nanna. "Take your hands off me. I'm fine. You make such a fuss about nothing."

Nanna's nose was bleeding, and she had a big bump on her forehead.

"Go get Dr. Sorensen," Gudrun said to Astrid. "I see his car; he must be home."

Astrid went next door and knocked three times, which was the signal that it was her.

Clara opened the door.

"Nanna fell. Is the doctor home?" she asked.

Clara called out for her husband. "It's Astrid; the old lady fell. Can you go next door?"

Dr. Sorensen announced that he was in the shower and that as soon as he was finished, he would come over to the house.

To Astrid's surprise, Aksel was home. When he saw Astrid, he tried to exit the room before she saw him. She was used to his strange behavior; it had been that way since they were teenagers. Gudrun explained to Astrid that years ago Aksel had a big crush on her, and because he was socially awkward, he didn't know how to express it. But Astrid thought that was not an excuse for his consistent rude behavior.

"Are you back from the retreat?" she asked, trying to make light of the situation.

"It's not a retreat; it's a workshop. To answer your question, no, I am not back. I came home to pick up some clothes."

Even as a young boy, Aksel looked like he had the weight of the world on his shoulders. He was a very smart student, top of his class, but as his teachers would say, he didn't put enough effort into his work. Aksel was more concerned with world events. He became obsessed with climate control and pollution. His mother had to stop him from watching the news. He took everything to heart and vowed to make a difference in the world, but as he got older, his anxieties held him back.

"Is this writer's workshop far from here?" asked Astrid.

"What's this? An interrogation?" he said annoyed. He could never look Astrid in the eye.

"Aksel, don't be rude," said his mother.

"Aksel is always rude to me," Astrid said.

He walked back into his bedroom and slammed the door.

"That's Aksel. Don't pay attention to him," said Clara. "He came to pick up warmer clothes, some towels, and a blanket. He is eager to get back to his writing."

Dr. Sorensen was ready to leave. "Come, Astrid, let's see what your grandma is up to," he said, twirling the end of his handlebar mustache.

Nanna was lying on the sofa with a warm cloth wrapped around her head. Gudrun had placed a pillow behind her and was giving her chamomile tea to sip. Dr. Sorensen examined her body, moving her limbs in all directions. Although she winced, he could tell that nothing was broken and she was only bruised.

"I think that we should order a walker for the pretty lady," said Dr. Sorensen. "It will help her move around easier so that she won't fall."

"Over my dead body will I use a walker," Nanna said in a surprisingly strong voice.

"Mama, no one will even know," said Gudrun. "It will just be for home, so you can walk around this area safely."

"I won't use it," she huffed. "The day I need a walker, it will be time to bury me."

The room fell quiet, as it wasn't worth an argument.

"I'll put an order in for a walker," Dr. Sorensen said. "If you use it as a clothes horse, that will be fine with me," he told Nanna.

Anton arrived back from work earlier than usual. He announced that the principal of the high school called him in and told him to take as much time off as he needed while the search for Anja was in progress.

"I will get my full salary," he said to Astrid. "There are still good people in this world," he added. "We must not forget that."

CHAPTER TEN

SARDINIA

Bar Sport wasn't open for breakfast yet when Luca arrived. Mario had just finished mopping the floors and was taking the chairs down from the tables. Stefano was setting up the bar. The air felt stuffy and smelled of old wine since the doors had not yet been opened to let the fresh air in.

"*Ciao*, Luca," Mario called out. "Do you want a coffee?"

"Yes, Grazie," said Luca. "Is Alessandro here?"

"Not yet. He usually gets here just after eight."

Luca looked at his watch and saw that it was exactly eight o'clock. He had not slept all night. He knew that he had to ask Alessandro a favor, but he also knew that this could be a bad idea. Alessandro was not a person to trust.

Luca sat at an outdoor table away from the door because what he needed to ask was not for anyone else's ears. Alessandro arrived on his Augusta Dragster Motorbike, revving so loudly that the cups and saucers on the table shook. He stopped just short of the sidewalk, removed his helmet, and threw it like a frisbee onto the handlebar. He ran his hands through his chin-length dark hair as he walked toward Luca.

"*Ciao*, my friend," he said. "Long time, no see."

I got a glimpse of you at the Saratiglia. Congratulations on your good race," Luca said.

"I wasn't crowned king, but I have to give others a chance," he said. "Mario! Two coffees and two prosciutto sandwiches."

"I've already eaten. Just a coffee," Luca corrected him.

"How's the trucking business going?" asked Alessandro.

"It's going. I'm always going somewhere," said Luca. He took a sip of coffee and took a breath. and asked, "What are you doing these days?"

"A little bit of this and a little bit of that," said Alessandro.

"You do know that Adela and I have a baby girl?"

"Ah yes, I bumped into Pia and she told me."

"We had some problems getting her papers," Luca said. He tapped the table with a fork.

"Why would that be?" asked Alessandro, taking a bite of his sandwich.

"There has been some confusion about her birth. Nothing important, just a mishap," said Luca.

"That can be a problem," said Alessandro. "What papers are you talking about?"

"A birth certificate," he said quietly.

"Why are you telling me this?" said Alessandro.

"I heard that you may be able to help us."

"Maybe yes, maybe no," he said.

"If the price is right?" asked Luca.

"It's got nothing to do with money," said Alessandro, taking a sip of his coffee. "I would only consider this for Adela; she's a good woman. Her father, Matteo, may his soul rest in peace, was a good man."

"How much?" said Luca.

"Twenty-five thousand euro," he said softly, looking around to see if anyone heard.

"I can do that," Luca said. He knew that there would be no bargaining.

"Half now and half when it's done," Alessandro said. "Call me and I'll give you a list of all the information that I will need." He wiped his mouth, threw the napkin on the floor, got on his bike, and roared away.

Luca had to calm down before he paid the check. He breathed slowly and drank a glass of water. He was still shaking when he left to go home.

When Luca came back, Signora Melis was making homemade pasta, tagliatelle, for dinner. Her hands moved adeptly like a piano player who had played music for so long that her fingers moved automatically.

The recipe was very simple, just eggs and flour. She poured the flour directly on the wooden table, creating a well, then she cracked four eggs and dropped them directly in the center.

"*Ciao,* Luca," she said as she was vigorously kneading the dough.

"*Bongiorno*, Mamma," he said, standing and watching her knead and punch.

When the dough was elastic, she set it aside for twenty minutes.

"Sit down," she said. "You look tired. Are you OK?"

"I don't know how to say this," Luca said. "So I will get right to the point. We have to get a birth certificate for Mira. We can't get her immunized or anything else until we have the right papers."

Signora Melis, who was now rolling the dough into a large flat disc with a long rolling pin, looked up, her brow furrowed. "Is that possible to do?" she asked.

"There is someone who can do this—birth certificates, passports, citizenship papers. Of course, it's illegal, so there is a risk involved, and that costs money. A lot of money."

While the pasta dough was drying, the Signora sat across from Luca and said, "How much?"

"Twenty-five thousand euro," he said, biting the inside of his cheek.

"*Dio mio,*" she gasped. "That's a lot of money."

"Can you pay it?" asked Luca.

"Who else will pay? Do I have a choice? Yes, I will pay."

She folded the dough in half, cut it into thin strips, and stacked enough portions for each person for dinner. She then dusted them with flour. "Well, one thing is for sure, we will eat well tonight," she said.

"*Grazie*, Mama, thank you," Luca said, relieved. He went to tell Adela the news.

Adela was sleeping on her side with Mira in her arms. They seemed to fit into each other like the petals of a rose. Luca marveled at how they were meant to be together.

Adela stirred, opened her eyes, and smiled at her husband. "Why are you looking at me like that?" she asked.

"Because I love you," he said.

"Come lie with us." She moved over, making space on the bed.

He lay down and moved his body into the curve of her back. He wished he could keep that picture in his head forever.

"Are you happy, Adela?" he asked, stroking her hair.

"Yes, I am," she said.

"Are you happy that I found Mira for you, for us?"

"I am. But I am afraid someone will take her away from us."

"I don't think that will happen," he said. "The birth certificate is organized. He agreed to do it. Of course, for a price."

"Who is going to pay?" she asked.

"Your mother. She agreed."

"My mother is the best mother in the world," Adela said.

"She sure is," he said. "And so are you."

"If I could be half the mother she is, I would be happy." She turned her head to face him. "Tell me one thing, Luca, does Mira come from another country?"

"Yes, sweetheart, she does."

"You never found her abandoned in the park?" Her voice rose with panic. "Please, Luca, it's better that I know."

"She was not abandoned. I can't tell you more. It's to protect you and Mira."

"Does she have a mother looking for her?"

"No, she does not have a mother looking for her. You are her mother, and you love her. Don't ask me anymore."

There was no peace in the room; even Mira became restless and started to cry. Although the sun was still high in the sky, darkness crept over the little family, covering them like a shroud where they lay still and sleepless, until Signora Melis called them for dinner.

Signor Rossi, Adela, and Luca rolled a forkful of pasta with meat sauce into their mouths and simultaneously sighed. Signora Melis's cooking was a balm for their souls. After a few sips of red wine, any problems they had dissipated.

"Mama, I married your daughter because of your cooking," said Luca. "I ate many meals at your house, and I figured if I could eat like this forever, I'm staying. That's the reason I proposed."

"So far, I haven't cooked for you Luca, so you don't know what the future will hold," laughed Adela.

"In the meantime, we will stay right here, close to your mother and her kitchen," Luca said.

"Remember how you insisted that my mother cook for our wedding? One hundred guests; that wasn't easy," said Adela.

"Of course, I remember. How could I not?"

"Your parents weren't happy with the food. They wanted it catered," said Adela.

"Nothing makes my parents happy," said Luca.

"It was a wonderful wedding, and all my friends helped. We cooked and baked for four days straight. It was a dream come true," said Signora Melis. "Papa would have been so proud."

Luca and Adela's wedding was put together in two weeks. Adela, just pregnant, didn't want to be showing at her wedding.

Early on a warm Saturday morning, the bride and groom, followed by family and friends, left from the Melis house for the short walk up the lane to the cathedral. Signora Melis had made Adela's brocade and silk dress. Pia had pulled Adela's long, wavy dark hair up with a wreath of white rose buds so that it cascaded down like silk over her shoulders. Luca wore a dark brown linen suit, with a crisp white shirt. He had grown a goatee for the occasion, promising Adela that he would shave it off right after the wedding. Together they made a handsome couple.

The ceremony was short and sweet. Padre Selvio made an extra effort because of Signora Melis's close bond to the church. He spoke slowly, enunciating each word from the bible and then in the sermon spoke highly of Adela's parents and their connection to the church.

Luca's parents were very quiet and shifted from leg to leg. They did not disapprove of their son's choice of wife, and they felt alienated from being a part of the wedding. That was no one's fault but their own. Adela and her mother had tried to include them in all the wedding plans, but they were not forthcoming. Adela confided in Signora Melis that she believed the reason for their indifference was that they didn't want to be asked for a monetary contribution. Signora Melis respected their wishes and did not ask them for a euro.

However, when the church ceremony ended, Luca's parents were given the honor of "Sa Razzia." A bowl of rice with wheat, salt, and coins—symbols of abundance and wealth—was given to them to scatter over the heads of the newlyweds.

Aperol aperitifs were served in the cathedral garden. Pecorino cheese, olives, and jams, in addition to myrtle liquors, were offered on platters to the guests. Luca had arranged for two white doves in a basket to be released into the sky after the ceremony. Pia had the honor of opening the lid. The doves, however, had a mind of their own. They huddled in the corner, refusing to move. Pia lifted them out with her hands and tossed them upward vigorously. They fell back down to earth. Everyone ignored what didn't seem like a good omen.

The guests made their way back to their cars, honking their horns while driving toward the beach for the wedding celebrations.

Signora Melis, with permission from the city municipality, had reserved space on the boardwalk by the beach. She had rented long trestle tables, white tablecloths, and chairs. With the help of her good friends, she strung fairy lights around columns that circled the area. Large glass bowls filled with wildflowers lined the length of each table, and white paper lanterns swung gently back and forth overhead.

"It looks like a fairyland," said her sister-in-law, who usually never complimented anything.

The ladies from the church, who were close friends of Signora Melis, set up the buffet tables with the food. There wasn't a space on the table that wasn't covered with hot casserole dishes.

Pia overheard Luca's parents complaining to each other that catered food would have been classier. She wanted to say something to them but decided against it. She also didn't want to upset the newly married couple.

Luca's colleagues from the trucking company played in a horn band, and along with an accordion player and an accomplished vocalist, the music motivated everyone to dance.

They danced with partners, they danced in groups, and they danced alone. It didn't matter as long as they were having a good time.

Even Signor Rossi danced. He was more comfortable with old Italian songs, but he could keep up with the younger guests. He even danced with Signora Melis, clasping her hand, with his other hand around her waist as they bounced up and down to the music.

Adela shot her mother a quizzical glance. She was not used to seeing her mother enjoy herself, especially with another man. She felt that Signor Rossi was overstepping his bounds.

"Mama is making a spectacle of herself," she whispered to Luca.

"Come on, Adela," he countered laughing. "Let her have some fun for a change."

"I don't think Oristano has seen such a happy wedding in many years," said Signor Rossi at breakfast the next morning.

"We won't forget the skinny dipping in the sea," laughed Adela.

"What does that mean?" asked Signora Melis.

"People swimming naked," said Adela.

"Pia made a name for herself last night," said Luca.

"What's new?" Adela said. "She and Alessandro fought, as usual. He was flirting with that girl from Cagliari, so Pia took off her dress and went running into the ocean."

"Silly girl," said Signor Rossi, taking a bite of a freshly baked croissant. "No boy is worth making a fool of yourself over."

"I think she just had too much to drink," said Luca. "Alessandro is bad news."

"I wish Pia would find someone nice," said Adela. "I feel sorry for her. She is always a guest at a wedding, never the bride."

Signora Melis added, "It always amazes me how good girls go after bad boys."

"I didn't," said Adela. "I went for the good boy."

"It's still early days; time will tell," said Signor Rossi.

"What? You don't think that I'm a good guy?" said Luca, annoyed.

"You still have to prove yourself," said Signor Rossi. "Only time will tell."

"He doesn't have to prove anything to you," said Adela. "I married him because I know who he is."

"Please, let's enjoy the day," said Signora Melis. "It's your first day as Signora Adela Pinna. Isn't that wonderful?"

CHAPTER ELEVEN

DENMARK

Astrid couldn't understand how the world was going on as usual while hers had imploded. People still went to work, children went to school, the buses ran on time, and the stores opened and shut, while her life was forever changed. She didn't know how she would survive one hour to the next.

Her phone call to her neighbor Dr. Sorensen was tough.

"Hi, Doctor, it's me, Astrid. Um ... my breasts hurt; I think I need medication to dry the milk."

"Hello, Astrid. Yes, I will give you something. I will send a prescription to your pharmacy, and they will let you know when it's ready, OK?"

"I was hoping that my baby would be found before I had to do this," she said, her words catching in her throat.

"I know. Better that we dry up the milk. You can always give the baby formula when she comes back."

"You think that she will come back?" asked Astrid.

"I don't have a crystal ball, but there is a good chance that they will find her," Doctor Sorensen said, measuring his words. "Denmark is a small country, and someone, somewhere, must have seen something. It's all over the news, and everyone is talking. That is a good thing."

"I am hanging on to hope," she said. "But it's so hard."

"Hang in there. We are all here for you," he said, ending the conversation.

After Anja was born and Astrid came home from the hospital, the home health visitor who came daily to check up on her and the baby suggested that she join a mothers' group.

"I will put you in touch with some moms in your area who have given birth around the same time as you," she said. "It's good to make friends with people going through the same experience as you are."

The home health nurse, an older woman with soft eyes and a warm smile, had just finished helping Astrid bathe Anja. She then showed her how to swaddle the baby tightly in a cotton wrap. She also helped the baby latch onto Astrid's nipple and offered suggestions on feeding techniques. The nurse was confident and experienced, and Astrid looked forward to her visits.

The nurse set up a meeting with Anja and a group of six new mothers who gave birth around the same time. These women were selected as a group because they all lived in the same area. Each mom would take turns hosting a meeting once a week in their home.

"Just a reminder," said the nurse when she called. "This is not about how clean the house is or how good the food is—it's about getting together to form a camaraderie with new mothers going through the same experience."

Astrid was nervous to go to the first meeting. She took a while choosing what she would wear. She still didn't fit into her regular clothes, so she decided to wear a loose-fitting striped dress. The get-together was in a house around the corner. She pushed Anja in her new stroller and walked at a quick pace.

When she arrived, the other mothers were already there with their babies. They seemed to have met before and were familiar with each other. Everyone was chatting and there were no awkward silences. They briefly looked up from their conversation and greeted Astrid warmly.

"Welcome," said a tall woman in a bright red poncho. "I'm Elsa." She pointed to her baby in her carrier. "This is Olivia."

"Hi, I'm Astrid and this is Anja," she said.

It didn't take Astrid long to relax. Everyone was in the same boat, all going through similar issues. They spoke about the hospital where they delivered the babies and compared notes on their birth experiences.

"How about we talk about the things no one ever tells you," said one mother sitting cross-legged on the chair.

"Yes! Like how painful the stitches are down below, and how I can't go to the bathroom," another mother said.

Everyone laughed.

"What about our boobs? Nipples are so sore and so raw," someone blurted out.

"*Ja*! Yes!" they shouted in unison.

"Shh ..." another mom whispered. "Let's not wake the babies."

"What do you all think is the toughest part?" A slim blonde woman asked.

"Hands down, the lack of sleep," answered Astrid.

"For sure," they all concurred. "We are exhausted."

They were all grateful that their husbands were given paid leave to share the baby's duties with them.

"We are so lucky. Other countries, I believe, don't give parental leave. The parents have to put their babies in daycare from early on," someone said.

Each week the host provided the food—finger foods such as sandwiches and pastries. There was also a selection of nonalcoholic drinks. Everyone had a story to tell, and everyone was interested.

Astrid told the group how difficult it was for her to conceive because of her infertility issues and how grateful she was to have Anja.

Ursula told a different story; her baby was born with Down's syndrome. They had known this from genetic testing early in her pregnancy. She said that although they were devastated upon hearing the news, not once did they consider terminating the baby and how happy they are that they made that decision.

One mother told them how easy her baby was—she fed him, put him down to sleep, and he didn't make a sound until the morning.

The other mothers were dubious that she was being truthful, but they kept quiet.

When Astrid's turn came to host the group, she had planned exactly what she was going to serve.

"I want to have a nice assortment of pastries and also cut up fresh fruit. I'm going to make little sandwiches with different spreads," she told Anton. "I won't have anything sweet, but maybe some salt licorice. You know how we are all crazy about that," she added excitedly.

"That sounds perfect," Anton said. "I will help you tidy up a bit. I know how crazy you get when guests are coming." He kissed her on the top of her head.

"Do you think it's going overboard if I buy little lavender soaps for the guest bathroom?"

"It is. But I will pick some up at the pharmacy tomorrow." He grinned.

Two days before the intended mothers' group, Anja was taken.

In the turmoil of the shocking event, Astrid forgot about the meeting. The mothers' group watched the news in horror and shock. Images of Astrid, Anton, and Anja were flashed all over the screen. It was so surreal that it took a while for them to process what had happened.

They immediately called each other but found it hard to get the words out.

"I can't believe this," they said. "This is a nightmare. What can we do? What can we say?"

They decided that it was not possible to call Astrid. There was nothing that they could say under the circumstances. All six mothers sat in silence and wept.

Each woman dropped off a casserole dish at Astrid's parent's home. They didn't know what else to do. They introduced themselves as Astrid's friends but couldn't make eye contact with Gudrun.

Jens and Gudrun were immobilized with shock, but their main concern was the well-being of their daughter. They made the effort to be there for her both physically and mentally. She was an apparition of despair. Her face was pale and thin, her eyes sunken, and her body stooped as if all the strength had been sucked out of her. Anton was bereft; he didn't have the words to describe what he was feeling. Everyone was rallying around his wife. He felt alone in his grief.

Clara went in and out of the Nielsen house for most of the day. She instinctively knew what to do and when to do it. She was a woman who was used to crises since her husband had brought many patients in need of a haven into their home. This time it was different. She considered the Nielsens as more than just neighbors; they were family.

Clara would have been a pretty woman if she smiled more; her furrowed brows and distressed eyes were those of an anxious person.

"Everyone has to stay strong for the baby's sake," she said to Anton and Astrid. "You can't fall apart. You have to conserve your energy for when she is returned safe and sound."

"But how?" said Anton.

"Make every effort to keep your mind and body strong. Help the detectives as much as you can. Focus on the present—one step at a time."

"We are trying," said Jens.

Clara's phone buzzed. She stood up and walked to the window.

"Aksel?" she said. "Are you still at the workshop? I transferred the money to you. You want to stay longer?" She then whispered, "The baby is still missing, this is a living nightmare. What do you mean they should have been more careful? That's a terrible thing to say."

Clara was visibly upset when she walked back into the room.

"He is on another planet," said Clara. "This book is just a lot of nonsense. He will never get it published."

"Did he say we should have been more careful?" asked Astrid, her voice rising.

"No, no, he didn't say that," Clara answered, clearing her throat.

"He is lazy," piped up Nanna. "A lazy, good-for-nothing, spoiled boy."

"Nanna, you be quiet," said Gudrun.

"She is right," said Clara. "We enable his nonsense. When he gets back, Harald and I are going to take steps to change things."

CHAPTER TWELVE

SARDINIA

Adela dug her feet into the soft pink quartz sand—it felt like grains of sugar between her toes. She sat alongside Pia on a blue and white beach towel under a matching umbrella. It was a beautiful day for the beach, the sky was clear, and the crystalline turquoise water was calm. Mira lay on her back in the shade, fixated on her toes. Her tummy was full, she was content.

Pia inhaled deeply on a cigarette.

"Don't blow the smoke near the baby," said Adela. "I wish you would give up this awful habit."

"It's my only vice," she said. "Leave me alone."

"I could name a few more but I won't," she laughed, kicking sand toward her friend.

"Smoking helps with my weight; I'm not constantly thinking about what I'm going to eat next."

"Why don't you take off your T-shirt? You have a bathing suit on, right?"

"I told you I'm fat. I am embarrassed. Not everyone is as skinny as you," Pia said.

The women enjoyed being together. They had known each other for so many years that they had a comfortable relationship. They almost knew what the other was thinking.

"You will be happy to know that I'm finally finished with that loser, Alessandro," said Pia. "He is not good for me," she added as if convincing herself.

"Good, it's about time," Adela said. "Do you want some water? I have plenty in the cooler."

A young family sat close by. The mother lay topless on her stomach, and the father was on a lounge chair, looking at his phone. The two young children were digging in the sand and ran back and forth to fetch water in their plastic buckets.

"I wonder if I will ever have that?" said Pia, looking at the family.

"Do you want that?"

"I didn't used to think so, but I'm changing my mind."

"That's a big revelation," said Adela. "Since when is this?"

"I'm looking at my life. I'm lonely; I have no one. You have Luca, and now Mira. It makes me feel that I am missing out on life."

Pia lifted Mira, placed her on her knees, and made baby sounds.

Mira studied her face, trying to copy her sounds.

"I can eat her up," said Pia. "Who wouldn't want a child like this?"

"If that's what you want, then go for it," said Adela. "Go and find yourself a husband and make a family. Do it."

"I've always wanted to be independent. I swore off marriage." She jiggled Mira up and down. "But I've changed my mind," she said. "It's a woman's prerogative to change her mind."

Luca was snorkeling in the ocean. The water was clear, and he could see fish in all colors of the rainbow darting in and around the rocks. You didn't need to dive deep to see life under the sea. Light hit the blue water, like schools of electrical eels traversing the ocean floor.

"Why don't you go and join Luca?" Pia asked. "I will watch the baby."

"As soon as he comes back, I will go in," she said. "I don't like to snorkel; I feel claustrophobic."

There were not many solo beachgoers that day, only families. Adela observed how happy they looked. These were the moments when one could put aside the worries of the world. She wondered how others would assess her. A young mother, a husband, and a baby. Adela couldn't dismiss the feeling of being an imposter. She felt that at any moment someone would point at her and yell, "That isn't her baby, she stole her."

"Do you want to have a swim?"

Adela looked up at Luca removing his flippers and drying himself with a towel.

"Yes, I do," she answered, standing up. "I'll just take a quick dip. Keep an eye on Mira. She is wide awake."

Adela walked toward the water, feeling Luca's eyes following her. She was petite, lean, and toned. Her hair, wild and curly, was twisted up with a tortoiseshell clip, tendrils escaping around her neck. Adela wore the smallest bright pink string bikini that showed off her golden tan. As a woman, she felt confident, but as a mother, a fraud.

"Tell me, Luca, did you get the birth certificate from Alessandro?" asked Pia.

"Yes," he said. " It's all paid for."

"Did he do a good job?"

"It looks very authentic to me," he said.

"Well, that's one less thing to worry about," Pia said.

Luca checked to see if Adela was still in the water, then he said to Pia, "You know the newspaper clipping that I have from Copenhagen?"

"Yes."

"It's missing from my drawer. It's the strangest thing. I had hidden it under my underwear."

"Do you think Adela found it?" she said.

"Who else? My mother-in-law never goes into our bedroom. We set boundaries and I have told her not to," said Luca.

"You told me that Adela commented about the foreign language on the baby formula container, and if she found the newspaper article, she has probably put two and two together."

"It must be hard for her to process. I feel for her," said Luca.

Pia lifted Mira and held her up in the air. "*Quanto sei bella!* How beautiful you are!" she said, swinging the smiling baby back and forth. She then kissed her on her cheek.

"Adela is coming," Luca said. "Don't say another word."

"The water was cold today," Adela said. "It's deep as you step in; there isn't a sand shelf like the other beaches."

"True," said Luca. "When Mira is older, we will go to the beach where the water is shallow."

"I'm starving," said Adela. "I will dry off, change Mira, and we can go and get something to eat at the little restaurant."

"Good idea," said Pia.

They first walked toward the showers to wash the sand off their feet, then to the cafeteria for a seafood lunch. Mira, wearing a little white sunhat, smiled in her mother's arms, her blue eyes twinkling like the ripples of the sea.

After an early dinner, they left the café. As they were walking toward their car, they came upon a group of men playing bocce ball. As they approached, they recognized Signor Rossi. He was bending down, studying the balls, and then with a big sweep of his arm he rolled the ball toward the small white ball, the pallino. Luca, Adela, and Pia waited until the ball came to a stop and called out to him.

"Signor Rossi! *Ciao*!" they said.

He stood up, shaded his eyes with his hand, and waved back to the group.

Luca then noticed that one of the players was his boss at the trucking company, Carlo Venuti.

"Good evening, Carlo!" Luca called out.

"Hey, Luca! Nice to see you and the family," he said. I'll see you tomorrow at work."

After they left, Signor Rossi turned to Carlo. "You know Luca?"

"Yes. He is one of my drivers."

"It's a small world," said Signor Rossi. "I rent a room in his mother-in-law's house. The young family lives there too."

"That's great," Carlo said. "Luca is a good guy. He is a hard worker."

They went back to playing the game. Signor Rossi was distracted and kept missing his mark.

"Pay attention. Concentrate," chided his teammate, Beppe.

The six men played a weekly bocce game on the beach, and although they wouldn't admit it, they were fiercely competitive. Whichever team positioned their balls closest to the small white ball, the pallino, won the game. The losing team had to buy a round of beer for everyone at the pub nearby.

The men drove in two cars to the center of town to their favorite beer hall.

"Well, I have to treat," said Signor Rossi. "I lost my touch tonight."

"Don't be a sore loser," said Beppe.

The men did not order anything to eat; hamburgers were not their style. They rarely ate out except on a Sunday after church. They would eat with their families at Mama Sofia's Trattoria only because her food had the reputation of tasting almost as good as at home. Salvatore Rossi drank a beer before heading back home for the best food in town—Signora Melis's.

"*Cin-cin*!" the men toasted, raising their beer mugs and clinking them together.

They took a long sip, smacked their lips, and wiped their mouths with the back of their hands.

Signor Rossi, seated next to Carlo, asked how his trucking business was going.

"Going," he said. "It's not an easy way to make a living. But it's stable."

"What do you deliver?" Signor Rossi asked.

"We truck mostly produce we grow in the area. We also drive cases of wine from local vineyards to customers. In fact, Luca is one of my wine delivery truck drivers."

"Where do you go?" Salvatore Rossi asked nonchalantly. He didn't want to sound as if he was prying.

"All over the EU. We go long-haul, that's where the money is. Not easy for the drivers. It takes many days and sometimes involves going on ferries over water."

"That's so interesting," Signor Rossi said, tapping his fingers on the table. "Is that where Luca goes?"

"Yup. He drives our Denmark route. A tough haul, but he is up for it. Never complains, and sleeps in the truck. Goes back and forth fast."

"I never knew," said Signor Rossi.

"He is married with a baby now. That's good." Carlo gestured to the waiter to bring the bill. "At least he settled down. He used to be a bit rough around the edges."

"He married a very nice girl: Adela Melis," Signor Rossi said.

"I knew her father, Matteo. He died way too young, a good guy. I used to spend time at his Tabacchi. Those were the good old days."

"Can you do me a favor?" Signor Rossi asked Carlo. "I need to know the dates that Luca was in Denmark in the last two months."

"Why would you want to know that?" he asked, taken aback.

"It's a personal issue. I'm trying to help my good friend Matteo's widow Signora Melis," Signor Rossi said.

"Do you think that Luca is cheating on his wife in Denmark?"

"Perhaps."

"I hope it isn't so, but I will give you his log schedules to check. Matteo, may his soul rest in peace, would be very upset if his daughter was being cheated on by her husband."

Signor Rossi went back home a worried man. He felt that something did not add up. A baby was missing in Copenhagen, kidnapped outside a restaurant around the same time a baby magically appeared in Oristano, Sardinia, to a young couple. Luca had been in Copenhagen during that time and had newspaper clippings of the abduction hidden in his drawer. He wondered how much his dear friend Signora Melis knew. Was she hiding a terrible secret? It seemed impossible; she was the kindest, most caring woman with a heart of gold. Signor Rossi couldn't shake the feeling that something was not right.

He had had this feeling once before in his life when he knew something was wrong, but he didn't act on it. He had gone through a heartbreaking incident because as a young man, he was naïve. He believed that *all* people were honest. He had learned a lesson the hard way. He should have believed that *most* people were honest.

Signor Rossi was an engineering student at the University of Naples when he met the love of his life. In high school, he was a shy boy and although intellectually gifted, he lacked confidence with girls. By the time he went to the university he had grown over six feet, and his features became chiseled like a marble statue. He never realized his allure until girls started noticing and flirting with him. Once that happened, his confidence soared, and suddenly, he became the life of the party.

At age twenty, Salvatore Rossi was still a virgin. He lived with his parents and younger brother in a two-bedroom walk-up apartment near the campus. He loved his father, but he adored his doting mother. She treated her sons like Gods. Nothing was too much for her to show her love and devotion to Salvatore. His meals, his laundry, and his room were immaculately kept by his mother—with the kindest grace. She enjoyed spoiling her sons and doing everything for them to enhance their well-being. Her life was her family, that was that.

Every Monday evening after classes, Salvatore had a calculus study group. He noticed one of the female students staring at him. Even when he caught her looking, she did not avert her eyes. From across the room, the two of them had a staring match—he finally conceded, lowering his eyes and blushing. She won.

After class, she boldly walked up to him. "You should be concentrating on your lesson more," she said.

"I can say the same of you," he answered.

Antonella was an engaging girl. Her features on their own were not perfect. Her nose was too long and her lips too thin. Her eyes were too close to each other but, together with her dark waist-long hair and curvaceous figure, she was a stunning woman.

It wasn't long before Salvatore found himself in bed with her. She lived in a rental apartment with three other girls. Antonella made up for Salvatore's sexual inexperience. She knew her way around a man's desires, and he picked up very fast. Although he didn't have anything to compare it to, he knew that this was better than anything he had read about or seen on a screen.

He started longing for the university studies to be over so that they could get together. Antonella was smart, savvy, and funny—he fell in love very quickly.

"I love you," he said, kissing the top of her head as she lay close to him in bed, where they spent most of their time together.

"I love you too," she mumbled.

Salvatore wasn't convinced that was true, but he didn't care. As long as she was with him, that was fine.

He took her home to meet his parents. After a big Sunday lunch of many courses, each more delicious than the others, his mother took him aside.

"She is not good enough for you, son," she said with a concerned expression he had never seen before.

"Mama, I really like her," he answered.

His mother's opinion was very important to him, so her statement was like a dagger to his heart.

Salvatore's father thought she was a decent, smart girl who knew what she wanted. Antonella was not afraid to speak her mind, and she often did.

"She is too opinionated," said his mother after she had left.

"That's a good thing," Salvatore said. "She doesn't let anyone push her around."

"Every time you talk, son, she talks over you and disagrees with whatever you say," his mother said.

"That's exactly what you do to me," said Salvatore's father.

"Yes, but you and I have been married forever, this is just a girlfriend. In the beginning, it should be sweet. If it starts out rough, it's only going to get rougher," said his mother.

Even though Salvatore did not want to accept his mother's opinion, he respected her observations. He stayed up all night weighing the matter of his heart versus the matter of his head. He had noticed certain characteristics of Antonella that bothered him. When morning arrived, he had made up his mind. He decided to break up with her.

After classes were over for the day, Salvatore called Antonella to tell her he was coming over.

"Please bring over a pizza," she said. "I'm starving."

When he got there, he found her crying.

"What is the matter?" he said, putting the pizza box on the table and taking her hand.

"I will have to kill myself," she said. "There is no other way."

"What are you talking about?" said Salvatore, taken aback. "What happened?"

"I am pregnant," she said, sobbing.

"How do you know?"

"I missed my period and took a test. It's positive."

"Am I the father?" he said in shock.

"What are you saying?" she cried. "Who else would that be?"

Even though Salvatore was in shock, there was no way he would let his child be born without a father. He asked her to marry him right away, and Antonella immediately accepted without further thought.

They had a small wedding in the church near Salvatore's home. His parents were not happy. His mother said, "I knew it. She trapped you."

Antonella was estranged from her parents. There was a rumor that she stole money from her ailing grandmother, but Salvatore could not verify that.

After the wedding, they moved into Salvatore's parents' home. His mother's heart softened. She declared that an innocent baby was coming into the family and that she would love that child no matter what.

Soon after, Antonella left the university because she felt too sick to get out of bed. Now that she was going to be a mother, she wanted to stay home and raise their child. She knew that Salvatore had already been offered a good job after he graduated.

It wasn't long after, early one Sunday morning before mass, that Antonella lay in the fetal position in bed, clutching her stomach and screaming.

"The pain," she yelled, writhing. "It's killing me."

Salvatore immediately went to borrow the neighbor's Fiat 500 to drive to the hospital.

"No, no!" she screamed. "I'm not going to the hospital."

"The baby," said his mother. "We have to try to save the baby."

Antonella jumped out of bed and ran to the bathroom; she locked the door behind her.

"Oh my God," she screamed. "Blood is coming out into the toilet. Lots of blood."

"Open the door," said Salvatore. He turned the handle, banging loudly, "Please open the door!"

Antonella refused. There was silence, interrupted by her deep breathing.

When she finally came out disheveled, there was no blood on her or the floor.

"I cleaned it up," she explained. "A big chunk of blood came out in the toilet bowl, and I flushed it."

Salvatore's father insisted that they call their friend Dr. Conti to come to the house despite Antonella's insistence that she didn't need a doctor.

He arrived soon after with his black bag. Dr. Conti went into the bedroom, examined a reluctant Antonella, and came out with an insightful expression on his face. The family knew something was not right.

"The young lady was not pregnant," he said flatly. "I fully examined her, and there was no indication of a pregnancy nor a miscarriage."

"What does that mean, *Dotore*?" Salvatore asked.

"Either this girl has psychological problems, or she is a liar," he said.

Divorce was not legal in Italy at that time, but after two anguished years it became legal, and Salvatore was able to divorce Antonella. They had already separated, but not before Salvatore paid her a large sum of money to leave. He never saw her again.

Signor Rossi became a skeptical man; he did not accept things as he was told. That was the reason that he had to find out the truth about what was going on with Adela and Luca's baby girl. Something was not right.

CHAPTER THIRTEEN

DENMARK

The long days took on a monotonous rhythm while the Larsen and Nielsen families waited to hear any updates on Anja. They were suspended in an altered reality. Anton, Astrid, and her parents moved around like robots doing the daily chores.

When the phone rang, Jens was the one who jumped up to answer. He mouthed that it was the police. They all stopped what they were doing as if in a freeze dance. They put down their cups of coffee on the kitchen table. With racing hearts, they took deep breaths to calm down.

"Hello," said Jens. "*Ja*, officer. We are not doing too well, as you can imagine." His knuckles tightened as he clutched the phone. "Any news? Leads?"

" A camera? What did it show?"

They all sat up straight, leaning in to listen.

"Not a clear picture? Too grainy. You couldn't see a face, just the back?" Jens repeated what the detective was saying. "Can you enlarge it? Uh-huh." Jens coughed and cleared his throat. "OK. Thank you for keeping in touch, we appreciate it. Please let us know if there is any progress."

"What did he say?" said Astrid. "What did he say?"

"There was a camera?" asked Gudrun.

"The 7-Eleven next door to the restaurant has a security camera. The video shows a figure, dressed in black, with a black woolen cap and a mask," Jens said with a quivering voice. "He or she picks up the baby out of the stroller and walks away."

"Oh my God," said Anton.

"My poor baby," Astrid cried.

"Did they see who it is?" asked Gudrun.

"They only got the back view, but they can gauge height and weight."

"A man?" said Gudrun, clasping her hands, rocking back and forth. "Why? Why would he take a baby?"

"The police believe it is a male, but it could be a female, they are not sure," said Jens. "With the technology that they have these days, they should be able to get a better image."

The family got very quiet. Astrid wiped the tears from her eyes. "I don't know how long I can go on," she said.

"Well, they now have something to work on," said Jens. "This is better than nothing."

They waited in anticipation, but there were no more reports from the police in the next few days.

It was the time of year when Gudrun pickled vegetables and herring to stock up the pantry.

"Today is pickling day," Gudrun announced, entering the kitchen. "We have to do the pickling," she said as if convincing herself. "Just like we do every year because this is our tradition and as true Vikings, we put one foot in front of the other to survive. All hands on deck! *Alle mand pa daek*!" she said.

Pickling was the last thing that anyone felt like doing. It took concentration and effort, which they didn't have, but they agreed it would be a much-needed distraction.

"I'll slice the red cabbage and beets," said Astrid in a monotone. She tied her apron on.

"OK. I will wash the cucumbers and carrots, and peel the onions," said Gudrun. "Jens, can you please combine the sugar, water, and vinegar in the big pot and turn on the stove?"

"I want to help, too," said Nanna. "I will prepare the green beans."

Gudrun brought out her little green book of canning recipes, *Den Gronne Sylteborg*, and propped it open on the kitchen center island. The pages were marked with stains and the corners folded in. She knew the recipes by heart, but displaying the book was part of the process.

Gudrun walked Nanna to the table and placed a pile of fresh green beans and a bowl in front of her. Nanna's expression showed that she felt important and needed. She pursed her lips with concentration as she picked up each bean and methodically broke off the ends. As the bowl filled, she was proud of her accomplishment.

There was silence in the kitchen while they peeled and chopped. Gudrun had the sole responsibility of pickling the herrings. She enjoyed the ritual of cleaning them. She cut off their heads, tails, and gills. Next, she slit open their bellies, removed the entrails, and scraped the insides well.

Gudrun rinsed the fish thoroughly while pulling the bluish skin off and then soaked the fillets in cold water. She had prepared sliced onions, bay leaves, pickling spices, sugar, and vinegar.

Lastly, she drained the herrings in the water, cut the fillets into squares, and filled the sterilized jars with all the ingredients. She found herself smiling as she finished.

"Do you remember when we found out that Astrid was pregnant? "Gudrun said.

"I remember it clearly," said Jens.

"We were over at your house for dinner on my birthday," she said to Astrid, "And you handed me a birthday present wrapped in a little box."

"Was it a scarf?" asked Nana. "She always gives me a scarf. Who needs so many scarves?"

"No, Mother, it wasn't a scarf. It was a photograph. 'Why is she giving me a photo?' I thought. Astrid told me to look at it again. And I did. It was an ultrasound picture of a tiny fetus," marveled Gudrun. "I shouted, 'Is this what I think it is?'"

"I had only found out the day before, so I was so excited," said Anton.

"We were all so happy. It took so long for you to conceive," said Jens.

"I have to believe that God would never allow anything bad to happen to this gift," said Gudrun.

"We want her back safe and sound," said Astrid. "That's all I can think about, having her back in my arms."

Gudrun started singing, quietly but strongly, "*Der er et yndigt land*, there is a lovely country."

The others joined in singing the national anthem of Denmark. It was a melody they knew well and the familiarity gave them comfort in their suffering.

They sang softly but in tune, as if they were praying to their motherland for help.

> "There's a beautiful country
> It says with broad beech trees …"

As they sang with tears in their eyes, Astrid wept with her head bowed while she continued chopping the red beets.

Then they all put down their utensils and clasped hands.

> "Hail any Danish citizen
> who gives what he can
> who gives what he can …"

Anton got up from his seat and walked toward his wife, wrapping his arms around her from behind and laying his head against hers.

"Our old Denmark will endure …"

When they stopped singing, they blew their noses and quietly continued with their chores. The boiling water became the background sound to their grief—bubbling and swishing as the steam rose, evaporating like their tears.

CHAPTER FOURTEEN

SARDINIA

The white chiffon curtains billowed softly from the cool breeze coming off the sea. Signora Melis had opened all the windows to cool down the house. The weather had turned warm even though it was still spring. The pink sky cast shadows of the setting sun against the whitewashed walls.

Signor Rossi was watering the plants with the garden hose; this was his evening ritual. The sunflowers lifted their heads, reveling in their nightly drink before tucking in their petals after darkness descended.

Rows of flowers in assorted bright colors shimmered from the droplets of water highlighted by the setting sun. Signor Rossi was proud of his sweet-smelling flowers and abundant vegetables that flourished under his care. The green artichoke buds were slowly opening, and the tomato plants shimmied up the wooden stakes almost ready to be plucked. But his pride and joy were the purple eggplants, shaped like small patent leather torpedoes, that he couldn't wait to harvest. Wild asparagus crept along the ground like belligerent children trying to escape. His triumph was the two majestic fig trees that spread out and threw shade in the garden. Their boughs, bent with dark purple figs ready to burst open, ushered in birds and bees. The neighbors were welcome to gather the surplus, and they did, bringing large baskets to fill. Signora Melis believed in sharing her blessings.

Signor Rossi came back inside, went upstairs, took a shower, and soon was in the kitchen for dinner with his wet hair slicked back.

"It's so quiet this evening; where is everyone?" he asked Signora Melis.

"The young ones have gone out to a movie, and Mira is sleeping."

He sat down at the end of the large wooden table which had become his assigned seat. Signora Melis always placed a fresh tablecloth with cloth napkins for every meal. The table was set with four settings no matter who was coming for dinner. It was not unusual for extra guests to join their meals, and the table was large enough to accommodate them. There was always a vase of fresh flowers in the center of the table picked from the garden. A bottle of still Smeraldina water and a pitcher of red wine was always routine.

Signora Melis placed a bowl of pasta fagioli in front of Signor Rossi, while he cut thick slices of freshly baked sourdough bread.

He slurped his first spoon of soup and smacked his lips. "This is so good," he said.

"*Manga*, eat up," Rosalia said. She rarely sat down to eat since she was usually too busy in the kitchen, but this evening she sat down with Salvatore.

"You're not eating?" he said.

"I'm not having soup; I'm too hot." She reached over for the platter of fish. "I grilled this grouper for us. It came straight off Mario's boat."

"You went to the docks?" he asked, sopping up the remainder of the soup with his bread.

"Yes," she said. "I was there at midday when the boats came back. That's the best time to get the fish."

"It is. Mario can get a little greedy with his prices."

"He dare not with me," she laughed. "I know how to haggle my way around a vendor."

"I wouldn't want to bargain with you," said Salvatore, smiling. He looked at Rosalia and for the first time, he noticed her fine features and pretty face. Her short dark hair was swept off her face with a bobby pin. She looked almost girlish, with a mischievous sparkle in her eyes. Rosalia must have been a beautiful young girl. Salvatore looked away. He didn't think it proper to have these thoughts.

Rosalia was fit too. She walked miles every day—to the market, to the butcher, to meet friends at the piazza. She rarely took a car or a bus. Her legs were robust and firm. Signor Rossi figured that the wine was clouding his vision and his mind so when he noticed the dark circles around her eyes, after a double espresso, he felt relieved.

Rosalia washed the dishes, while Salvatore cleared the table. He cleared his throat and asked casually, "Signora, is there anything you would like to tell me about baby Mira?"

She swung her head to face him a little too fast. "Why would you ask me that? You can see for yourself that she is a happy and healthy child."

"That she is," he said, rubbing his chin. "I had a strange dream the other night that you told me that she was adopted."

"Oh nonsense." Rosalia stared at him, eyes wide open, unblinking. "That is crazy. Are you drunk?"

"Maybe a little," he said. "She just looks so blonde and different."

"That is ridiculous. We have blondes in the family, and I have blue eyes. I'm hurt that you could even say that. I'm not going to tell the children. They would be furious."

"Please forgive me, Signora," he said, getting up from the table. "Please disregard my comments. It must have been the wine talking."

Signor Rossi thought it best to go upstairs to his room. His original thought of staying downstairs and watching TV with Rosalia wasn't a good idea.

Signora Melis was up earlier than usual, just before sunrise, as she had a busy day ahead. This was the time of year when the family pulled together to can fresh tomato sauce to last for the entire year. Signor Rossi had already picked piles of plum tomatoes and transported them in a wheelbarrow to the back porch. The area was large, with concrete floors and a retractable canvas awning to protect them from the intense heat. There were two standing electric fans turned on high to move the still air and offer relief in the stifling heat. Three large steel tables were pushed together to hold the giant tubs for the tomato sauce. Extra-large aluminum pots were filled to the brim with bright red plum tomatoes bubbling on the outdoor gas stove. Signor Rossi, in charge of those pots, stirred the sauce like a wizard mixing his brew. The steam rose like the mist before a storm. He added chopped garlic and then dribbled olive oil into the mix. Luca was stationed in the kitchen sterilizing the jars in boiling water. Adela poured steaming tomatoes into huge colanders, where they drained and cooled down. They all wore old, stained clothes for the occasion and their cloth aprons were splashed crimson red.

Signora Melis ladled the tomatoes into an electric machine whose main function was to crush and puree them into a thick velvet sauce. She added a spoonful of salt and a pinch of sugar into the terracotta bowl. Luca lined the sterilized jars in a straight row on the table, placing a large basil leaf inside each one. Signora Melis filled the jars with the tomato sauce to the top and sealed them tightly with a rubber screw cap.

She smiled with satisfaction as she surveyed their labor of love. Forty jars of magic sauce are to be placed in the cellar for the winter months. The accomplishment put everyone in a good mood. Signor Rossi sang while he worked and Adela chose not to chastise him, after all, he was very helpful on this mission. Pia was on baby duty, holding Mira on her lap. She was happy not to be involved in making the sauce because her long acrylic nails would have been ruined.

Luca's cell phone buzzed. He saw that it was Alessandro and knew from history that this would not be a pleasure call, although Alessandro had been paid in full for services rendered so no further communication was necessary.

Luca wiped his hands on his apron and pressed the green button. He listened, biting his bottom lip.

"Bastard," said Luca. "*Stronzo*, asshole." He pressed the off button.

Adela noticed her husband's grim expression. "What's the matter?" she asked.

"I just had a call from that piece of shit, Alessandro, and guess what?"

"What?" she said, gesturing for Pia to come and listen to the conversation.

"Alessandro said that because he took such a big risk forging the birth certificate, he feels that he deserves extra compensation. He wants eight hundred euros a month or he will go to the authorities."

"How can he go to the authorities when he committed fraud? They will arrest him," said Pia, shifting Mira to her other hip.

"Anonymous," Luca said. "He will make an anonymous phone call."

The three of them stood silent.

"Can we ever have a good day?" asked Adela.

"He has me by the balls," said Luca.

Signora Melis called out to them, "We are finished. This calls for a celebration. I have tagliatelle made with our fresh sauce. Thank you, my children!"

"What about me?" said Signor Rossi, carrying the jars down to the cellar.

"*Grazie mille*, Salvatore." She looked him straight in the eye. "Loyalty means everything to me."

CHAPTER FIFTEEN

DENMARK

Astrid felt that wherever she went everyone was looking at her. Whispering, shaking their heads—feeling sorry for her. It wasn't that they were saying anything bad about her, but she felt their pity, like a net thrown over her, encasing her anguish. People she knew averted their eyes when they bumped into her at the local grocery store. They never asked the questions—"How are you doing? Has your baby been found?" They figured if there was good news it would be reported in the news, or worse still, if there was bad news everyone would know about it.

Astrid pushed her shopping cart up and down the aisles at the local supermarket. She randomly threw items into her basket. She didn't pay attention to the different brands of pasta, sauces, sugar, or canned goods. She just reached for the closest one and put it into the cart. In the fruit and vegetable section, she chose red apples and dark green avocados solely for their bright colors. As she was reaching for an orange, someone called her name.

"Astrid?" said an American accent.

She turned around to face Carly, the exchange student who was now a pariah in the town. She was dressed in exercise gear—a crop top, tights, and sneakers.

"Do you want to grab a coffee at the coffee shop in the store?" Carly asked.

Astrid nodded her head, and they both walked toward the snack bar. They ordered coffee and a pastry and sat at one of the round tables.

"I'm going back to the States in two weeks," said Carly. She took a big bite out of her pastry filled with a custard filling. "Yum," she said.

"Where are you staying?" asked Astrid.

"At a bed and breakfast on the circle."

Astrid took a sip of her coffee. "Are you happy to be going home?"

"It's bittersweet," said Carly. "I like being here, but I do miss my family and my dog." She licked the cream and crumbs off her lips. "Would you be interested in coming to a yoga retreat with me before I leave?"

"Tell me more about it," said Astrid.

"There is a yoga retreat close to the white cliffs in Mont Klint that I found on a website. It looks really good."

"I took yoga before Anja was born," said Astrid. "I found it beneficial for my mental health. What makes you want to go to this one?"

"This looks like the pure yoga philosophy, centering oneself, balancing mind and spirit. The pictures show beautiful nature, lots of green forests, and incredible views of the cliffs." She continued, "I am free until I leave, and I think that this would be good for me to regroup before I go back."

"I am interested. I have to find inner peace while waiting for Anja to return," Astrid said. "I don't know how I can go on anymore without breaking down."

"I will email you all the details. We will have to go within the next few days," Carly said. She stood up, kissed Astrid goodbye on both cheeks and left.

Astrid usually took time to weigh all the pros and cons of any decision she ever made but with this retreat, she impulsively decided to go. She felt there was nothing to lose and maybe something to gain.

When she told Anton, he wasn't too enthusiastic.

"I don't think this is the right time for you to go," he said.

"There will never be the right time," Astrid countered.

"What if there is some news of Anja?"

"I will only be gone for four days. I will be contactable on my phone the whole time," she said to convince herself as well. "It's only a two-hour train ride from here."

Within two days, they were on the train from Copenhagen to Mont Klint. The final stop was Vordingborg St. where they would get off and then take a taxi to the Zen Wellness Sanctuary up in the hills.

Astrid and Carly were in an otherwise empty compartment. They sat in silence looking out the window, and as green fields flashed by, they both felt a sense of relief, letting go of pent-up stress and anxiety. The train gained speed, making a hypnotic clanking on the rails, and as the motion shook them from side to side, Carly began talking in a monotone voice.

"I didn't intend to have an affair with Erik. It was the last thing on my mind," she said as if taking a sip of truth serum. "I have never been attracted to older men. He is older than my father. It started with him telling me how pretty I am and how mature I was for my age. Then he said how much he enjoyed talking to me because I am much more open and curious than the girls of my age in Denmark. Erik started buying me little gifts—a pearl necklace, a pair of gold stud earrings, and then a book of his favorite poems. I felt special; no one had ever paid me so much attention."

"It's a pity that it couldn't stay platonic," said Astrid. "I feel that Pastor Johansen is a hypocrite. He preaches the sanctity of marriage. He should know better than that."

"I was also to blame," Carly continued. "I started wearing more revealing clothes around him—pulled my T-shirt a little lower, hiked up my skirt, that sort of thing."

"Yup, you knew what you were doing. Didn't you care about his wife?"

"Truth be told, I didn't."

The train inspector came through the door, stopping at their seats to check their tickets.

"Good day ladies," he said.

"Hi!" answered Carly. "How long do we still have to go to the station?"

"About another fifty minutes," he said.

"We are going to Mont Klint. I believe the cliffs are stunning," she said. "Have you ever been there?"

He grunted and walked away.

"Did I say something wrong?" Carly asked Astrid. "He seemed annoyed by me."

"Americans on the whole are more outgoing and friendly to strangers. Over here, people have to get to know you before they feel comfortable making small talk."

The taxi driver, however, didn't seem to mind chatting when they were driving up to the retreat. He said in Danish, "These things are a waste of time and money. You can't learn to be happy; it has to come naturally. Either you are a happy person or not. It is your choice, but no one can teach that to you."

"What did he say?" Carly asked Astrid.

"That we are wasting our time and money coming here."

"I hope that he is wrong," Carly said.

He dropped them off at the wooden arch with a big sign—Welcome to The Enlightenment Journey of Peace and Love.

A large clearing of pressed gravel circled by tall trees leaning into one another was the first thing that they saw. Scattered around were clay circular huts with thatched roofs that blended into the forest like camouflaged soldiers. But it was the majestic white clay cliffs soaring down to the deep blue Baltic Sea that took Astrid and Carly's breath away.

"Wow," said Carly. "I could just stand here forever and look at this view."

Two young women in white robes came out of the main hut to greet them. Despite the coarse terrain, they were barefoot, wearing red threads around their ankles. They clasped their hands together and dipping their heads slightly, they greeted them. "Namaste," they said in unison.

Astrid and Carly, carrying backpacks, followed the women up the path to a steep stone stairway. They clung onto the uneven wooden railings, treading carefully so as not to slip. The two women ahead sauntered up like two mountain goats. They stopped in front of a hut identical to the others. A curtain of colorful wooden beads that click-clacked in the wind was the sole door.

"We don't have doors," said the girl with a long braid as if reading their minds. "We want the flow of good energy passing through the room without barriers."

There were two bamboo mats on a linoleum floor, each with a blanket, a flat pillow, and a small table and chairs. There were four wooden shelves for clothes. The windows were wide open, and you could see the backdrop of the stark gray and white sweeping cliffs.

The young women told them that after they had settled in, they should make their way back down to the main hall for dinner. They then left.

"This is very basic," said Astrid, folding the minimal clothes that she had brought with her on a shelf. "It's very stark. I expected a little more comfort for what we paid."

"This is part of the experience," said Carly. "They want us to focus on our inner selves and not material things."

A gong chimed loudly. Astrid and Carly made their way down the steep steps toward the main house, clutching onto the railings. They entered a large, domed ceiling hall filled with about fifty people. Everyone was dressed in comfortable clothes, flat leather sandals, and lots of leather bracelets. Their scrubbed faces gave off a heavenly glow. They looked ready to expand their consciousness. Everyone sat cross-legged on the bare floor. Astrid and Carly, feeling exhausted and haggard, joined the group to sit cross-legged on the floor. Men dressed in orange robes flanked Mother Serenity as she entered the arena. They then stood silently in a straight line. Mother Serenity, the guru leading the retreat, waited for one of the men to blow his conch shell before raising her arms and circling them above her head. "I usher in peace and serenity," she said. Her followers answered, "We are open to receive your calling."

She was a tiny woman in a white toga that wrapped around her small frame. Two things surprised Astrid and Carly. The first, that Mother was wearing high-heeled boots, and the second, her face was fully made up including fake eyelashes. She did not look as natural and earthy as her followers. She had jet-black, waist-long, straight hair that was parted in the middle, covering most of her features like a veil. Astrid and Carly shot each other a look. She was not what they were expecting.

She introduced herself as Mother Serenity with an accent that they later learned was Brazilian. Mother went on to explain that higher conscience is only possible if one cleanses all the mental baggage that bogs us down. That was the mission of this retreat, to reveal the barricades that hold us back from the embodiment of a pure soul. She then invited everyone to get a plate, line up at the buffet, and enjoy the farm-to-table offerings.

"Remember, we are what we eat," she said. "In the following days, you will only be eating raw, vegan, organic food sourced from only the most spiritually pure soil and blessed water."

"I was hungry until I saw the food," said Carly to Astrid, surveying the platters of raw vegetables and fruit dishes.

"I don't like raw beetroot and kale," said Astrid. "And everything here is either beetroot or kale."

Most of their fellow diners had been coming to EJPL every year for years. They were intrigued that it was Astrid and Carly's first time.

"You can call yourselves virgin truth seekers," a man with colorful beads braided in his goatee told them.

After lunch, a yoga class was held outdoors in the large courtyard. Everyone had brought their yoga mats. The yoga instructor stood facing the yogis on a low bench. He focused on the fundamental yoga poses, flowing from one to the next with the correct breathing. A group of four instructors went around checking for effective alignment. Astrid did OK, but Carly was stopped and realigned most of the time. The instructor corrected her quietly and gently with his hands and her face turned red from embarrassment.

They were led to the meditation room, a domed windowless structure. A young man with dreadlocks was playing a flute. The same yoga instructor from the class guided them through relaxed meditation to enhance their increased mindfulness. This was followed by a silent meditation. Astrid found it hard to switch off, her mind going back to the day that Anja was taken. She felt clammy and faint. Trembling, she stood up from the floor and left the room.

Carly followed after her.

"Are you OK?" she asked her friend.

Astrid was sitting on a low wall with her head down, breathing deeply. "I am not feeling too well," she said. "My mind won't turn off."

Carly offered her cold water and then after a few sips, poured the water over Astrid's head. Wet droplets dripped down her face onto her T-shirt.

"That feels a little better," Astrid said. "Maybe this wasn't such a good idea coming here. My head is just not right."

"Try switching off your thoughts," said Carly. "That's the purpose of meditation—to be in the moment without thinking." Carly massaged Astrid's shoulders.

"Could you just switch off?" asked Astrid.

"I was just thinking how hungry I was," she laughed. "I've never eaten so little before."

They then made their way back to the hut and collapsed on their mats, falling into a deep sleep.

There was a rhythm to their days: yoga, meditation, meals, and then the group gathering at sunset. As a bonus, Mother Serenity offered a one-on-one private consultation at an added cost. Both Astrid and Carly decided to make a reservation. They had heard that Mother's intuitive insight was a powerful gift.

Carly went first. She was told to go to the last hut on the right of the dining hall for her consultation with Mother Serenity. When she entered, Mother pointed to a sofa for her to sit on. Carly suddenly felt nervous. Her pulse was beating in her ears, and the palms of her hands were sweating.

"No need to be nervous," said Mother Serenity, throwing her hair over her shoulder like a cape. "I'm not going to bite you."

Carly exhaled and tried to relax. "I'm not nervous," she said, twirling her hair.

"Do you have a reason to be?" asked Mother. She handed Carly a hand mirror and told her to look at herself closely. "What do you see?" said Mother.

"I see me," said Carly, feeling foolish.

"Do you like what you see?"

Carly knew how to play the game; she had been to retreats before.

"I love what I see," she said boldly. "I am a beautiful person. A giving person with a kind heart."

"Interesting," said Mother as if looking through her. "I see a girl with a mask. A façade. She pretends to be good but it's all an act. She is not so good; in fact, she's bad."

Stunned, Carly said, "Excuse, me? That's a horrible thing to say. You don't know me at all."

"I've been observing you the last few days, and it's all about you. You don't care about anyone's feelings as long as you are doing OK."

"I didn't come here to be insulted," said Carly, getting up and striding out the door.

"The truth hurts!" Mother Serenity called out loudly for her to hear.

When Carly came back to the hut she was gulping with tears falling down her cheeks.

"What's wrong?" asked Astrid, alarmed.

"That woman is such a bitch," sobbed Carly. "Who does she think she is?"

"Why? What did she say to you?"

"She told me that I'm a horrible person."

"That's crazy," said Astrid. "She doesn't know you. You came here to be lifted up, not squashed down."

Next, it was Astrid's turn to meet with Mother Serenity. She walked through the door full of dread.

Mother looked up from her laptop and gestured for her to sit down.

"My friend was very upset after she came back from seeing you," said Astrid.

"I don't discuss other people's issues," said Mother. "So, what brings you here, to this retreat?"

"It sounded like a good idea, and I had some free time."

"I don't think that's the truth," said Mother. "I wish you all would just tell the truth," she said, spelling out each letter. "That's what this is all about."

"I came here to find some peace, and it's not working. That's the truth," said Astrid.

"I know who you are, Astrid Larsen. I do watch the news. I am sorry that your baby was abducted."

Astrid was speechless.

"You came here looking for answers," said Mother Serenity. "There are no answers."

"What am I supposed to do?"

"Accept. Accept that your child has gone. Accept that she may never come back. Only if you accept the worst can you go on with your life."

"How can you say that? I will never accept that she is gone forever. Don't destroy my hope that she is still alive and well."

"She may be alive and well, but until you accept the worst-case scenario, you will never heal."

"You know what I think the truth is?" said Astrid. "The truth is that you are a charlatan and a scam." She approached Mother and spoke in her face. "You just enjoy breaking people down. I would have expected compassion from you. You should practice what you preach."

Mother Serenity picked up her phone and told security to come immediately.

Astrid raced out and ran up the stairs to the hut. She burst through the curtain of beads and told Carly to start packing.

"You were right, this woman is a monster. How dare she play with people's emotions! We are leaving right now."

"What did she say to you?" Carly asked.

"She destroyed my hope that Anja is still alive. She said I should accept the worst-case scenario."

They threw their belongings into their bags and rushed down the stairs, then through the arch with the welcome sign. No one called out after them. They got into a cab and headed for the train station. Both women were shaking, but no more tears were shed.

CHAPTER SIXTEEN

SARDINIA

Signor Rossi sat under a red awning in the shade at the La Campagna restaurant on Piazza Eleonora. He ordered risotto ai frutti di mare, rice with seafood. He felt the need for comfort food. The waiter, a young sprightly fellow with a shaved head and yellow sunglasses, put the hot bowl of rice mixed with clams, shrimp, squid, and mussels on the table. Signor Rossi drank only sparkling water because he needed a very clear mind. He finished eating the risotto so quickly that by the time the waiter brought the breadbasket, his plate was empty. Usually at lunch, he could sit for two hours.

"Signore, what's the rush?" asked the surprised waiter, removing his dish.

"I have things to do in Cagliari," he said.

"It's not good for your digestion to eat in a hurry. Can I bring you a small grappa, so that you won't get heartburn?"

"No, no, thank you so much. Just a double espresso please."

Signor Rossi rocked back and forth in anguish. He had been up all night debating whether he should go to the main police office in Cagliari to file a report about the baby. But what would he say? That he was suspicious about the circumstances of Mira? Show them the Danish newspaper cutting and tell them he believed this is the missing child? Explain how he found the newspaper clipping hidden in the father's drawer? How could he convince them of his suspicions that this baby turned up out of the blue after the mother's prior pregnancy ended with a stillborn birth? It sounded so far-fetched that the authorities would think that he was crazy.

He downed his espresso in one gulp, left the money on the table, and hurried off toward the train station.

The train ride to Cagliari was one hour. Signor Rossi tried to close his eyes and take a nap, but a mother and a little girl were sitting in the seats facing him and the girl didn't stop asking if they were there yet. Signor Rossi was becoming annoyed that he couldn't sleep. He opened one eye and glared at the mother.

She smiled at Signor Rossi. "Please excuse my daughter. She is very excited to meet her father for the first time."

Signor Rossi didn't feel like getting into a conversation, but the woman was very persistent.

She bent toward him and spoke softly so that her daughter, who was drawing pictures on the tray table, couldn't hear.

"I only just found out who the father of my child is," she said. "Through DNA. It's amazing how far medical science has come. He denied it for years, but he was court mandated to take the test. He now wants to meet her."

"So you think this is a good thing?"

"Well, yes, she is four years old. and this is a good time for her to get to know her father."

"I wish you good luck and hopefully everything works out well for you and your daughter."

"Are we there yet?" asked the girl.

"Soon," replied her mother. She picked up the drawing her daughter made of a mother and a child. "Where is the daddy?"

"There is no father," the girl answered.

"Why?"

"Because I don't want a father," she said.

The mother looked up at Signor Rossi, rolled her eyes. and slowly shook her head. She said, "I do need your good luck after all."

As soon as the train pulled into the station, Signor Rossi got off. He knew exactly where the *stazione di polizia* was because he had been there before for various small matters. The building was a long walk from the train station, but Signor Rossi was fit and he was used to walking. The difficult part was opening the police station door and going in. He felt conflicted.

He walked up to the glass enclosure where a woman sat at a desk. He was the only person there. She was concentrating on her computer and paused reluctantly. Looking up at him over her glasses, she asked if she could be of help.

"I'd like to talk to an officer please," he said casually, as if he did this often.

"What is this about?" she asked quizzically.

"It's a private matter," he said.

She pointed to the clipboard on the ledge and told him to sign in with his name, address, and telephone number. She then instructed him to wait for an officer to come and get him.

He didn't sit down; he paced back and forth. Signor Rossi could see uniformed policemen through the glass behind the receptionist, some sitting at desks, some standing, others on their phones. They looked tired, with dark circles around their eyes. Men who had seen it all, men who were burned out. He was surprised when a woman with dark hair pulled back in a long braid strode toward him.

"*Buon giorno, Signore,*" she said, "What can I do for you?"

"I need to discuss something with you," he said. "Can we go somewhere private?"

"Of course," she said. "Follow me." He followed her through a double door to an office that was bare except for a desk and two chairs. The plaque on the door read Detective Pirelli.

"What do you want to tell me?" she said, sitting down at her desk, putting her chin on her clasped hands.

Signor Rossi sat down, reached into a leather portfolio, pulled out the folded piece of newspaper, and handed it to her.

She unfolded the paper, scanning it over before she looked up. "What is this?" she asked.

"Um, this is from a newspaper clipping in Denmark," he said.

"Yes, I see. How is this connected to you?"

"I think I know something about this," Signor Rossi said, his voice cracking.

"Please explain," she said, looking over the paper.

"I'm just concerned about that baby. I can't come to terms that someone just took a child."

"Yes," she said. "People do strange things. Why are you showing me this? Do you know anything about it?"

Signor Rossi cleared his throat and looked down at the floor. "I was just wondering what if that baby turned up in Sardinia. Would anyone know?"

"You came all the way from Oristano to tell me that? How did you get that newspaper cutting?"

"I found it somewhere," he said, wiping the sweat off his brow with his shirt sleeve.

"Look Signore, please don't waste my time. Either you know something or you don't. We don't play games here." The detective tapped a pen on the desk. "I'm going to make a copy of this newspaper cutting, and while I'm gone, make up your mind what you are trying to say."

She left the room. Signor Rossi got up from his seat and bolted out the door.

The woman at the desk called out after him, "Signore! Signore! You must sign out."

But he was gone. He speed-walked back to the station, not stopping for oncoming traffic. He was not aware of the cars beeping their horns. "Idiot!" They called after him. "Do you want to kill yourself?"

Only when he sat down on the train did he allow himself to breathe normally and calm down. He realized that he didn't have it in him to tell them of his suspicions.

He felt ashamed of himself; he was a coward. But then again, he had to ask himself, was he one hundred percent sure? Because if he wasn't, he would ruin the lives of a family whom he had grown to love, and he could not do that.

CHAPTER SEVENTEEN

DENMARK

Astrid took the shortcut down the alley, behind the brick commercial buildings, to the meditation park. Since she had returned from the retreat, she had found this little haven of solitude in the heart of the city. She was wearing her Doc Marten ankle boots and each step echoed on the cobbled path.

It happened so fast that her brain only registered the event after some seconds. She knew her mind had not played tricks on her when she felt the knife prick into her neck.

"Don't make a sound," a man said, holding her head with one hand and the knife with the other.

He had a ski mask over his head and was dressed in black. He forcibly pushed Astrid along the path, pushing his legs against hers as if in a choreographed dance. Then he stopped at a white van, slid the back door open, and wrapped duct tape around her eyes and mouth. He then bound her wrists behind her back. She was violently pushed onto the back seat. Astrid's mind floated out of her body, hovering over the scene as if observing a horror movie.

The man slammed the van door shut, jumped in the driver's seat, and they drove away. Astrid's mind was blank; she did not count the stops, she did not try to guess the route, she just waited for the next scenario to unfold.

Suddenly the van stopped, he jumped out, slid the door open, and pulled her out. He marched her up a short path, pausing to unlock the door, before forcibly pushing her inside. She fell to the ground, He ripped off her blindfold and the tape off her mouth, and while she lay there reeling from the pain, he spoke for the first time.

"The baby is here; see to her. I can't deal with this anymore," he said, removing the woolen covering from his face and tossing it on the floor.

As Astrid's eyes adjusted to the dark, she saw a wooden box at the side of the room. In it was Anja. She lunged toward the makeshift crib. Anja was lying with her eyes open but not making a sound. Astrid gently lifted her baby into her arms.

"My baby, my baby," she cried, clutching Anja to her chest. She wanted to melt her into her being. She kissed her head, her face, her neck. "Mama is here, mama is here," she repeated over and over. Anja relaxed her tense body, pushing herself into her mother's chest. She felt the familiarity of the touch and smell of someone who loved her dearly. Astrid could feel that she was smaller and frail, but the only thing that mattered was that she was alive.

"Why Aksel, why?" she turned to ask him as he stood stiffly to the side. "Aksel, why?"

"You are a bitch, that's why," he said.

"What did I ever do to you that you could punish me like this?"

"You fucked up my life, bitch, that's why. You always thought that you were better than me."

"Why did you bring me here now?"

"Something isn't right with this child, and I can't take this anymore. I want to punish you, not myself. Why should I have to put up with this crap while you run around as free as a bird?" He was pacing the room and talking very fast.

"I wanted you to suffer, so I took what I thought would be the worst suffering for you. It backfired. You were running around having a great time. Going to retreats and having fun while I am locked in here with a screaming baby who pees and shits herself all day. What is wrong with this picture?"

"Everyone will be looking for me, don't you get that?" she asked.

"Let them look. They haven't found the baby, have they? This house is remote, and no one will look here. You also have to stop talking. You just don't know when to shut up."

"I will help you," Astrid said. "Can I give her a bottle?"

Aksel took her into the kitchen. On the counter, there were cans of baby formula and bottled water. The kitchen was tidy and fully stocked. This must be the family's house at the lake. Astrid had never been there, but she knew that the Sorensen family spent time there in the summer.

Astrid was so happy to be with Anja and to see that she was alive that she didn't care about anything else at that moment.

"She does feel warm, maybe she has a fever," Astrid said.

"She has fucking diarrhea," he said.

Astrid put a towel on the unmade bed and removed Anja's diaper. She did have diarrhea and a very bad rash.

Aksel ran out of the room, retching. "The main reason you are here is to change her dirty diapers," he said, blocking his nose. "I underestimated the stench of that poop."

"You will have to get some baby cream for her rash," Astrid called after him.

"Don't give me orders," he said. "I will go to the store when I want to."

"Who looked after Anja when you went shopping?"

"I left her here. The kid can't walk. She was perfectly fine."

It suddenly occurred to Astrid why her baby wasn't crying. Anja didn't make a sound; she just lay there. She had probably cried so many times and never got a response, so she learned that crying doesn't help. Astrid felt bereft when she worked out the reason for Anja's silence. At four months old, she didn't smile, make eye contact, or make any sounds. Astrid was so angry at Aksel but she knew that to keep him stable, she would have to play his game.

Aksel locked the door when he left for the pharmacy. He took Astrid's phone away and put it in his pocket. He warned her, "Don't even think about escaping. If you do, I know where you are at all times, and I will do bad things to you, the baby, and your family. Do you get it?"

Astrid nodded.

"There is food in the fridge if you are hungry. Help yourself," he added as he was leaving as if she was a house guest.

Astrid sat hunched on a chair rocking Anja back and forth. She held her so tightly that she wished that she was back safe in her womb. Anja drank very little of her bottle and was lethargic. Astrid looked around the room. The windows were caulked and shuttered. There were three narrow open slat windows along the living room ceiling. The doors were locked and bolted from the outside. The cabin was on a large expansive lake. The closest neighbor was a few miles away.

Astrid knew that her parents must be frantic about her whereabouts. She would have been back home hours ago. They were worried about her well-being and kept checking on her. One evening she had overheard her mother say to her father, "If Anja isn't found, or if the news is bad, I am worried what Astrid might do."

"I know," said her father. "She loves Anton but that is not enough to sustain her."

So when Astrid did not come back from the meditation garden, her parents feared the worst. They called the police to report a missing person. The police knew right away who she was.

"I don't think it's a coincidence that both the baby and now the mother are missing," said the police officer to his colleague.

"It is possible that the same person who abducted the baby may have taken the mother," they concluded.

Once again, the officers went door to door asking questions to see if anyone had seen anything. Once again, they checked the security cameras all around the area. This time they found nothing.

As soon as the news broke, reporters went wild with their theories. It was on the news channels and in the newspapers and on everyone's minds.

"Was it the same kidnapper as the baby? Was the mother involved in this scheme? Was the father the culprit?"

Anton was a broken man. First, his child and now his wife was missing. He was still on leave from his teaching job. He felt that he had no purpose any longer. As the days went by, he sat around bickering with his in-laws. They too were suffering. Their emotions were raw. They tried to stay calm, but their anxiety would get the better of them and they would explode.

"Can't you chew with your mouth closed?" Gudrun said to Anton.

"Who cares about my chewing at a time like this?" Anton answered, chewing louder.

"Leave the boy alone," said Jens. "Stop picking on him."

Gudrun got up from the table, threw off her apron, and ran crying to the bedroom, slamming the door.

"I can't take this anymore," said Anton. "My life is over."

The Sorensens came over as if for a funeral visit. They sat hunched on the sofa as if life had been sucked out of them too.

"First the baby, and now Astrid. What has happened to the world?" said Clara, blowing her nose on her handkerchief.

"They will find them," called out Nanna from her rocking chair. "God won't let you down."

"Shut up Nanna!" yelled Anton. "You don't know anything."

"Don't be rude to Nanna," said Gudrun. "Why don't you get off your butt and go look for your wife and daughter."

Anton leaped up and walked out the door, slamming it on his way out. He jumped on his bicycle and rode away.

"Everyone's nerves are shot," said Dr. Sorensen. "We just have to focus on getting them back. There has to be a reason. People don't just disappear."

"The entire police force is out looking for them. There have to be some clues," said Jens. "I know my daughter; she is very smart. She will find a way to figure her way back."

"If we just knew that Astrid was with Anja, we would feel better. That is my prayer, that the two are together and alive."

Clara's cell phone rang.

"Ugh, it's Aksel again," she said, looking at the caller ID.

"Aksel, this is not a good time," Gudrun said. "Terrible things are going on. Astrid is now also missing. What? All you can think about is money. Do you need more money? God damn it, Aksel, I am getting sick and tired of this. I will transfer cash to you, but please come home. We need you here for moral support."

"I can't argue about money with him now," Gudrun said to them. "I don't have the energy. Once he publishes his book, he can pay us back. We spend our time worrying about petty things like Aksel not getting a job. but now with Astrid missing, that's so insignificant."

CHAPTER EIGHTEEN

SARDINIA

It started as a regular weekday but then things took a turn for the worse. Signora Melis was doing the weekly laundry. She refused to use a washing machine and dryer. "Nothing can wash better than my hands," she insisted. She held up her hands to show their size and strength, twirling them back and forth.

"These hands have washed loads of washing my whole life and look how smooth and soft they are," she boasted.

Signora Melis got pleasure out of rinsing and ringing out the fabrics with her bare arms and strong hands. She scorned the dryer even more. "The sun is the best dryer of all," she said. "Nothing can sanitize as well as nature, and nothing compares to the smell of the laundry from the sun. No perfume can beat that."

"Oh Mama," begged Adela, "You must be the last person on the island that doesn't have a washing machine or a dryer. It is so much more convenient. It would save you so much time."

"What else do I have to do?" asked Signora Melis. "I enjoy it, so leave me alone."

The clothes, the sheets, the towels, and the cloth diapers were pinned with wooden clothes pegs on nylon rope in the back garden. Signora Melis could predict the weather patterns by the way the clothes moved in the wind. When they were still, it meant there was no impending rain; a light flutter was a forewarning that the weather could change. If the laundry escalated to a wild flapping, that signaled the need to immediately hurry out and bring everything inside. Her children argued that most of her day was spent agonizing over the plight of the laundry getting wet in the rain. They asserted that a drying machine would free her up to worry about other things. But Signora Melis would not budge, she was stubborn. Even Signor Rossi tried to change her mind. There were many times when she was in town and called Signor Rossi frantically to bring the laundry in from the storm. There were other occasions when she wasn't home that she called her neighbor to check the weather conditions back home. The family finally gave up. There were more important issues to worry about. The plight of the laundry was not worth fighting about.

The family was at home when there was a loud knocking at the door. Three loud raps, then the door flung open. Three men in uniform called out, "Polizia coming through!" They rushed into the room, standing in a half circle. Signora,

Luca, and Adela, carrying Mira, rushed out to see what the commotion was about.

The first officer spoke. "We have reason to believe that this baby may not belong to this family."

"What are you talking about?" said Signora Melis, turning white.

"Who are the parents of this child?" the second officer asked, pointing to Mira.

"We are," said Luca, pointing at himself and Adela.

"There must be a mistake," said Adela. "You have come to the wrong place."

"We have been sent by Interpol to collect DNA samples from both of you," he said. "We also need a sample from the baby."

"We refuse to allow this," said Luca in a loud voice.

"We don't need your permission," said the officer. "You have to cooperate, or we will remove the baby from the house."

He told the family to sit at the dining room table. One of the officers brought out a kit for each person. They swabbed Luca, Adela, and Mira inside their cheeks. When they were done, the officer explained that as soon as they had the test results, they would call them to come into the headquarters. Without further explanation, they left.

Adela started screaming hysterically. "*Dio mio*! They will find out the truth! They will take Mira away. What are we going to do?"

"Stay calm," said Signora Melis in a shaky voice. "Don't upset the baby."

Luca, pacing up and down said, "It's going to be fine. It will work out. Stop screaming."

"Don't you tell me what to do!" Adela yelled. "It is not going to be fine. This is all your fault."

"You went along with it, didn't you?" he said. "I did this for you."

"This is not normal," she cried. "We are not normal." She banged her head on the table.

"Stop!" yelled Luca. "You can't lose yourself like this."

Luca crouched in front of Adela and took her hand in his. "Later, when we are alone, I am going to explain the whole story and tell you exactly what happened."

"What story? What else happened?" asked Signora Melis.

"You are making me so nervous," said Adela. "Please just tell me and get this over with."

"Not everything is what it seems," said Luca. "Everything I did, I did for you, Adela."

"The DNA. They took our DNA," she sobbed. "They will know."

"It must have been Alessandro who called and snitched on us," said Luca. "I refused to pay his blackmail money and he warned me that he would call the police anonymously. He obviously did."

The family was immobilized, waiting for the DNA test results. They could not function from fear. Signor Rossi, who had not been home at the time of the police raid, stayed in his bedroom. He agonized over whether the detectives had followed up on his lead or if in fact Alessandro vindictively reported them.

Adela was not speaking to Luca. She did not look angry; she looked hurt. She would not let anyone near Mira and held onto her like a lifeline, and she vowed to herself that no matter what truth would unfold, she would rather die than let her baby go.

A few days later, the police called to tell Luca and Adela to come to the main office for the test results. On the bus ride there, they never said one word to each other. Luca reached out to hold Adela's hand, but she vigorously pulled away.

When they arrived at police headquarters, the receptionist led them to a small office. A man in plain clothes was seated at a desk. He nodded to them to be seated in front of him. There was a sealed manilla envelope on his desk.

"We have the DNA results of your baby girl," he said as if talking about the weather. This man was experienced in delivering important news—he kept his voice emotionless, monotone, and clear.

He lifted the envelope and tore it open. The phone rang. He rattled off a short conversation about nothing to do with their case. Luca's legs were shaking so rapidly that the table shook. Adela's back was wet from perspiration.

The officer took a sheet of paper out of the envelope and looked up at Adela.

At that moment, a woman walked in. "Officer, what would you like to order for lunch?"

"The usual," he said. "Just tell them that the prosciutto must be thinly sliced."

She walked away.

"Let's continue," he said. "Adela Pinna, the DNA results support the position that you are not the biological mother of baby Mira Elisabetta Pinna."

Adela did not flinch; she swallowed and hung her head.

He then turned to Luca. "Signor Luca Pinna, the DNA results support the position that you are the biological father of baby Mira Elisabetta Pinna."

"I told you," Luca whispered to Adela.

"Everything you told me before was a lie," she said. Adela stood up, turned toward her husband, and slapped him in the face. "If you told me the truth from the beginning, I wouldn't have suffered as much," she hissed.

The officer stood up. "No, no. Stop that. This is not the time or place for your emotions to get the better of you," he said. "Good day to you both. Here are signed copies of the test results and I wish you good luck." He shook Luca's hand, but Adela put her hand behind her back.

When the couple got home, Signora Melis walked up to them, trying to read their expressions, but all she saw were blank stares. Signor Rossi rushed over with panic written all over him.

"What did the tests say?" Signora Melis blurted out.

Luca looked as if he had just run a marathon and was still recovering.

Adela went straight to her room and shut the door.

"Mama, please sit down. I have a long story to confess to you. Adela already knows it all." He didn't know what to do with his hands. First, he clasped them back and forth, then with clenched fists, he tapped his chest.

Signora Melis and Signor Rossi looked at him as if he had gone mad.

"Should I leave the room?" asked Signor Rossi.

"You can stay," said Luca. "But please let me explain everything and don't interrupt me until I'm finished."

They both sat down, waiting with bated breath.

"I have something to tell you that you won't expect," Luca said. "I am the father of Mira."

They both gasped.

"How can that be?" Signora Melis asked. "Then who is her mother?"

"Pia is her mother."

"You are lying! Why would you say such a thing? That is impossible." Signora Melis turned white.

"Early in Adela's pregnancy, Pia discovered that she was pregnant too."

"Don't say it. Don't say that. I can't take this," Signora Melis said, blocking her ears and closing her eyes.

"Signora, stay calm," Signor Rossi said, rubbing her arm.

"I slept with Pia. There I said it. You can throw rocks at me later," said Luca. "I am Mira's father."

"You had sex with Pia when my daughter was pregnant with your baby?" said Signora Melis.

"Yes."

"Piece of shit," she said. She picked up her glass of water and hurled it at him.

"*Stai calmo*," Signor Rossi repeated and jumped up to pick up the glass and wipe the water off the floor.

"When my baby boy was stillborn, Pia came up with a plan. She intended to give up her baby for adoption since she was not in a position to keep it. I agreed to that."

"Traitor!" screamed Signora Melis. "My daughter was carrying your baby and you were screwing her best friend."

"Let me finish. I beg you," said Luca. "So, Pia decided to give us her baby. Instead of giving it up to strangers. I am the father, and she wanted Adela to be the mother. There was a big problem though. Adela would never agree to take a baby under these circumstances—a baby born from me having an affair with her friend."

"Of course not," said Signora Melis "My daughter would never take that baby. After all, she has morals. You obviously do not."

"She took a stranger's baby. Is that the morals she has?" Luca shot his mother-in-law an exasperated look. There was silence in the room. "We thought this would be the best solution to our situation."

"I can't believe that you are so stupid," said Signor Rossi. "I have lost all my respect for you."

"What did Adela say when you told her this?" Signora Melis asked as she stood up to walk toward Adela's room.

"Mama, wait … I haven't finished."

"Don't ever call me Mama again," she said, sitting down again. "I am not your mother anymore. I would like to know when you had all this free time to cheat with Pia?"

"Pia sometimes accompanied me in my truck to deliver wine in Denmark. One thing led to another. These were overnight trips. We slept in the cab above my seat in my truck. When we got to Germany, we took the ferry over to Copenhagen."

"I still can't believe that you both betrayed my daughter."

"You can't make this stuff up," said Signor Rossi in shock.

"I treated Pia like a daughter, and she lived in our home. How could she do this to Adela?" said Signora Melis, crying.

Signor Rossi went up to her and put his arms around her.

"Signora Melis, it's a terrible story, but you know what? This is better than thinking that they had abducted a child from innocent parents. I mean, none of us believed the story that Luca found an abandoned baby lying in the bushes."

"Why did you want us to believe that the baby was from Denmark? It doesn't make sense," said Signora Melis to Luca.

"We were in Copenhagen at the time that a baby was kidnapped from outside a restaurant. Pia and I saw the news on TV and the headlines in newspapers. It was big news when we were there." Luca gulped to take in air. "Pia came up with an idea. She said that instead of giving our baby up to strangers for adoption, she would be much happier giving the baby up to me and Adela. This way she would be able to see the baby and she felt it was the best situation. The biggest problem was that we knew that Adela would never accept that Pia and I had an affair and take the baby as her own. That would be impossible. So, we hatched what we thought was the perfect plan."

"Slow down, you are talking too fast. I can't understand," Signora Melis shouted.

"We would make Adela think that I had kidnapped a baby in a foreign country. She knew that I traveled to different countries. I bought cans of formula and diapers in Denmark to fool her. I thought I had covered all the details."

"Is that why you had the newspaper clipping of the kidnapping in your drawer?" asked Signor Rossi.

"How do you know about that?" Luca said.

"I found it, Luca. You are not as smart as you think."

"Why would you be looking in my drawers?"

"The day we had the flood, remember? I was packing away your clothes and I found it," said Signor Rossi.

"I placed it in my underwear drawer hoping Adela would find it when she packed away my laundry," Luca said. "After Pia had the baby girl in a small country hospital near here, we brought the baby to Adela. I know you aren't going to believe it, but both Pia and I wanted Adela to be happy. We thought a baby would help heal her from the loss."

"That is the most ridiculous plan I have ever heard," said Signor Rossi. "Just because you wanted to hide your affair, you played with your wife's and family's emotions."

"You are an idiot!" Signora Melis screamed at him. "A crazy fool. You should be locked up in a mental institution."

"I beg for forgiveness," said Luca.

"Adela now knows the truth. She loved Pia like a sister. How could you both do that to her?" Signora Melis cried, blowing her nose. "You are not God. You can't play with people's lives."

"I thought, and I was right, that Adela would be so happy to have a baby that she wouldn't ask too many questions," said Luca. "You didn't ask any questions either," he said to his mother-in-law.

"Do you have the DNA proof that Pia is the mother?" asked Signor Rossi. "You have lied so much, how can anyone believe you?"

"Pia will have the test soon," he said. "Just to prove it to everyone."

"You told Adela all of this?" asked Signora Melis. "Last night?"

"I told her everything. She is hurt and angry; I can understand that. I tried to explain to her that this is better than what she had thought. Mira is not an abandoned child; she wasn't taken from anyone. I am the father, and she can legally adopt Mira. It will all work out fine."

"What about your relationship with Pia?" said Signor Rossi. "Do you think you can cheat on your wife, and voila! All is forgiven?"

"I love Adela," said Luca. "I want our marriage to work. It's over between Pia and me."

"That is up to Adela," said Signora Melis. "I am very disappointed in you, Luca. Once trust is broken, it's hard to fix."

"I wonder what happened to that baby in Denmark?" said Signor Rossi. "They haven't found the perpetrator. It is a tragedy, and I feel very sad for the parents."

CHAPTER NINETEEN

DENMARK

Astrid fell asleep with Anja cradled in her arms. Aksel came back with the shopping.

He looked down at the sleeping duo and said, “Such a peaceful sight. Mother and baby sleeping together.”

Astrid opened her eyes and for a minute wasn’t sure where she was. Then it became clear.

Aksel continued, “I shouldn’t be good to you, Astrid. You made my life a misery in school.”

“How?’ she asked.

“When we had the graduation school dance, I asked you to dance, and you said ‘no.’ Do you realize how hurt I was? Everyone was laughing at me.”

“Aksel, I don’t remember you asking me to dance. I would have liked to dance with you. Are you sure you asked me?”

"I didn't ask in words. I stood close by, and you knew what I meant. You just disregarded me as usual. Always treating me like dirt."

"I asked you to ride to the park many times with me, and you refused, Aksel. I wanted to be friends with you."

"That's what you say now, but then you would whisper bad things about me to your friends. Do you think I didn't see?"

"I never meant to harm you. I am very close to your mother and father; you are all like family to me."

"You mocked me my whole life. You would tattletale to my mother about me. I know. Do you think that I am stupid?"

"I never mocked you, Aksel. I've always admired your intelligence. I told your mother how smart you are."

"No. You didn't. You told her how weird I was and how the other school kids thought I was crazy."

"That's not true."

He took out the baby rash cream from the pharmacy bag and threw it hard at Astrid, hitting her forehead. She could feel blood running down her face.

She wiped her forehead with her hand, realizing how dangerous he was.

"I have a lot of anger in me," he said. "You don't know half of it. I have thought many times of just finishing you off."

"I don't understand," she said. "I don't know what you mean."

"The book. The book that I'm writing. The story that everyone keeps on at me about finishing. Do you know what it is about?"

He didn't wait for her answer.

"The book that you don't stop mocking me about," he stood close to her and loudly said into her ear. "You are going to love this! It's all about you."

"Me?"

"It's the log that I have detailed over the years of all the terrible things you have done to me—a chronicle about your cruelty. I have a full record of every time you insulted me. I have spent many nights thinking about retaliation. Then I came up with my plan. The most I could hurt you with is by taking away your baby. To put my plan in motion, I had to figure out how to take the child. I followed you for a long time, spending hours and hours watching your every move. I knew that you went to that park, I knew that you would stop for a bite, and I figured you would leave your baby outside since you have done that before. I am brilliant. No one knows how brilliant I am.

"After I brought the kid home, I realized that even with all the research I had done on babies, I didn't anticipate how hard it is to take care of them. I was punishing myself!"

Aksel went to the refrigerator and took out a can of Coca-Cola.

"Do you want one?" he asked Astrid.

She shook her head.

He opened the can, took a sip, and continued the story. He sat down on the sofa next to her.

"I realized this brilliant plan isn't working for me. Why should I be punished for taking care of your baby? That's when I figured that having you here would be easier for me. I haven't come up with the end of my novel. Do I keep you or do I get rid of you?" he laughed. "I will have to play it by ear."

Astrid was very quiet; she had nothing to say.

"By the way, can you make meatballs?" he asked her. "I'm dying for meatballs like my mother makes in a sauce. There is chopped meat in the fridge. It would be great if you would make us some."

"I can make meatballs," Astrid said.

"We can pretend that we are a family," he giggled. "Oh, I have something I want to address with you. It's been on my mind."

"What?"

"While I have you here, I think it would be a good idea if we had sex."

"What do you mean?" Astrid said softly.

"What do you mean, what do I mean? Come on Astrid. Sex. I have my needs. I am a man, after all, even though you don't think so."

"About the meatballs, let me start cooking," said Astrid. "I will feed and change Anja first."

"No, you won't," he said. "My needs come before hers."

Astrid went into the small kitchen. It was an open plan, and she could see the living room from where she stood. She took out the meat from the refrigerator, unwrapped the plastic covering, and placed it in a bowl. She took out an egg, and then an onion, which she began chopping into small pieces. She then left the room.

"Where are you going?" he asked.

"To the bathroom," she said.

She headed toward the bathroom and saw that Aksel had removed the door. The bathroom was open so that she could not be private. Astrid could see Aksel sitting at the kitchen counter rolling himself a joint.

Very quietly, she took out a wrapped chunk of chopped meat from her pocket. She pulled down her panties. She squeezed the blood from the meat into the lining of her underpants. She sat on the toilet pretending to pee, pulled her panties back up, threw the rest of the meat into the toilet bowl, and flushed it away.

Astrid made her way back to the kitchen. She washed her hands and started rolling the meatballs. She browned the onion in a pan on the stove and then added the seasoned meatballs. She transferred the meatballs into a casserole dish, adding a white sauce that she had made, and placed the dish in the oven to bake.

"That smells good," Aksel said.

Anja was waking up; Astrid went to pick her up and gave her a bottle. She held onto her mother's hand while taking small sips, then stopped and looked up at Astrid and smiled. Astrid's heart leaped this was the first time that Anja had smiled since she had been taken.

"The meatballs are baking, we will eat in a few minutes," Astrid said to Aksel.

After she fed and changed the baby, Astrid took the dish out of the oven. She had made rice as well. Aksel had set the table—he had rolled red napkins and placed them in the wine glasses just like a romantic dinner table set for two.

"Come and eat," she said.

"This is *hygge*, so cozy, like a real family," he said.

She put his plate in front of him, and he poured red wine into each glass.

"*Laekkert*, yummy," he said, tasting the meatballs. "Almost as good as my mother's."

"She is a great cook," said Astrid. "I wonder how your parents are doing?"

"They are doing just fine. They are relieved that I am away."

"I'm sure that they miss you. Your parents adore you, Aksel."

"I'm a big disappointment to my father. He wanted me to follow in his footsteps and become a doctor. I'm not the son he had hoped for."

"You will have to go back home soon," said Astrid. "They worry about you."

"They would be very surprised to know that we are together," he chuckled. "Wouldn't that be a shock? Their biggest wish was for you and me to get together and now we are. When you married that idiot, that put an end to that dream."

"Why don't you call and tell them that we are together? That would make them very happy."

"I'm not crazy, Astrid. Please don't think you can play games with me."

After the meal, Aksel went into the living room and sat down on the sofa. "Sit here," he said to Astrid, patting the seat next to him.

"I can see you better if I sit across from you."

Aksel got up and walked toward Astrid, pulling her by her arm. "You sit where I tell you," he said, shoving her down next to him.

He leaned over and tried to kiss her on the mouth. She instinctively pulled away. Aksel grabbed her ponytail and pulled her head toward him, forcing his mouth on hers. He reached down for her leggings, and shoved his hand inside the band, pulling them down.

"I have my period," Astrid said.

"Don't lie to me," he said.

"I'm not lying. I'm bleeding—a lot. I was going to ask you to get me tampons."

He pushed her back on the sofa, ripped off her leggings, and pulled down her panties. He saw the blood pooled inside.

He jumped up. "Ew, disgusting. *Foj*! Yuck!" he yelled. He started retching and ran toward the bathroom. She could hear him making vomiting sounds.

When he reappeared, he was pale and had a wet face from splashing water on himself.

“It’s disgusting. Don’t come near me,” he said. “Go and take a shower.”

He went to his bedroom and slammed the door.

CHAPTER TWENTY

SARDINIA

Trust is a very unique trait. You share your vulnerabilities with someone, breaking down barriers when you feel someone has your back, so if you are betrayed, a piece of you is destroyed.

Adela's trust was broken, not only by her husband but also by her best friend, the most important person in her life besides her mother. The DNA results came back as expected. Pia was Mira's biological mother.

"Adela, you must be strong," said her mother. "Mira is your baby and that is that."

"It is very hard for me mama. Now every time I see Pia with Mira, I can't help thinking that she is the real mother, and she knows that."

"You have the adoption papers legally signed, and Pia has relinquished her baby to you. She is the biological mother; you are the real mother. It was a decision that she made of her own free will. There are many open adoptions where the birth parents can play a part in their children's lives. That is up to you. But you are the mother, and of course, Luca is the father."

"It makes me so overwhelmed and confused," she said. "I agree that it is better than me thinking that my baby came from a mysterious situation."

"We are also not innocent," said Signora Melis. "We were in denial about the baby's circumstances. What were we thinking?"

They sat in Mama Sofia's Restaurant where they ate because Adela insisted that her mother take a break from the kitchen. Mama Sofia's food was homemade, fresh, and delicious. There were only eight tables in the tiny space, and if you didn't get there early, you couldn't get a seat. It was the neighborhood's favorite place to eat where diners sat for hours figuring out their lives. There was something about the crooked walls, the bunches of garlic and salami hanging from hooks on the ceiling, and the smell of ragu bubbling on the stove that made one want to linger longer.

"Hello, my friends," said Mama Sofia, approaching the table. "Why so serious?"

Mama Sofia was a big woman with a large head and a mammoth chest that made you want to lay your head on that softness and fall asleep. Just like the comfort food that she served, she was the comfort haven of the neighborhood. She knew all the answers to life's problems, and the community regarded her as a soothsayer who could predict the future of relationships.

She placed a steaming bowl of Malloreddus alla Campidanese in front of Signora Melis and Adela—pasta in tomato sauce with sausage and a hint of saffron.

"This will put a smile on your face," she said. She pulled up a chair. "Tell me, what's going on?"

"Our family is in turmoil," said Signora Melis. "Adela just found out that Luca was cheating on her with Pia." She sighed.

"That fatty?" said Mama Sofia. "She must have some tricks up her you know what."

"I don't think I can forgive him or her," said Adela. "But our baby is involved in the mess too."

"Forgive him but don't forget about it," she said, drumming her fingers on the table. "Men get an itch that needs to be scratched, sometimes by other hands beside their wives. Aldo scratched many times. Of course, now, he can't lift a finger, not even a tickle. Nature solves everything with time," she scoffed.

"With respect Signora," said Adela, "That is old-fashioned thinking. Today you have to have trust in a marriage. Both the husband and the wife shouldn't cheat."

"Papa cheated on me," said Signora Melis.

"Mama! That's not true; how can you say that?"

Signora Melis shrugged her shoulders. "There are things about him that you don't know."

"Pia is my best friend. You both know that she was raised in our home like a sister," said Adela.

"That is true," said Signora Melis. "I treated her like a daughter."

"That's true. Those are different circumstances," said Mama Sofia. "Adela, you must decide for yourself if you want to cut her out of your life. Luca has to cut all ties with her. You are a beautiful, strong young woman, you call the shots, it's in your hands."

Mama Sofia stood up, kissed each woman on the cheeks, and went back to her kitchen.

"Right now, I can't bear Luca to touch me," Adela said. She then looked her mother straight in the face. "Papa cheated on you! I am so shocked."

"I was suspicious," said Signora Melis. "He always came home late from work. I thought nothing of it, but when I did his laundry, I knew something was up. His clothes would smell of a perfume I didn't recognize, and there were the telltale lipstick stains."

"That is terrible. What did you say to him?"

"I never said anything. What was the point?"

"How can you be so loyal to his memory? You pray for his soul every day."

"We had a good marriage, Adela. I have many happy memories. Your father was good to me and you. I'm not going to let some 'flings' destroy those memories," Signora Melis said.

They left the restaurant just as the town was waking up from the afternoon siesta. After lunch, the adults and children took a long nap. The stores would close, and the shopkeepers headed home. Silence fell as if the townsfolk drank a sleeping potion. Three hours later, those same shutters would be pulled up, the church bells rang, and the town woke up refreshed to face the rest of the day.

Adela had left Mira asleep under the watchful eye of Signor Rossi. He did not partake in the afternoon siesta but preferred to do his gardening. Since the recent revelation of the baby's roots, Signor Rossi felt a great sense of relief. He was taken aback that he had misread the signs, but the way things turned out was for the best. He also was comforted to know that it was not him who had betrayed the family, but money-hungry Alessandro.

Signora Melis greeted Signor Rossi as she came in the door. Adela went to check on the baby.

"We ate well at Mama Sofia's today," said Signora Melis.

"That is the only place I will eat in town," he said. "Would you like an Aperol Spritz?"

"That would be nice," she said.

Signor Rossi took out the bottle of Aperol from the liquor cabinet. He filled two glasses with ice, poured in some cold sparkling wine, filled the rest of the glass with the bright orange Aperol, and added a splash of soda water. He garnished the rim of the glass with an orange wedge as the finishing touch.

He carried the cocktails out to the patio where Signora Melis was seated.

"Voila!" he said, handing her a drink. They each lifted their glasses, clicked them together, and said, "*Cin cin*! Cheers."

Signora Melis took a sip. "This is so good," she said.

"This is so wonderful," he said.

They sat in silence, listening to the birds calling out to each other. The church bells rang. Life can be good if you make the right choices.

CHAPTER TWENTY-ONE

DENMARK

Severe trauma causes the brain to play crazy tricks for survival. The sun crept in through the shuttered windows awakening Astrid. She lay on the couch with Anja in her arms. Astrid's heart was filled with joy to see her child. However bad her circumstances were, finding Anja alive trumped them all.

She traced her fingers over Anja's forehead, down her nose, and over her mouth. Anja looked up at her mother and smiled. Each day since they were reunited, the baby's expressions were coming back to life. She even started crying again.

"Shut her up," yelled Aksel from his room. "I'm trying to sleep."

"Can I close your door?" asked Anja, "So we don't disturb you."

"*Ja*," he said.

She softly closed the door.

Astrid carried Anja to the kitchen, filled her bottle with water and three scoops of powdered formula and while it heated in the microwave, she made herself a coffee from the Nespresso machine. She sat down at the wooden table in the dining room and fed Anja. Axel's laptop was open, and she glanced at the screen. It was page 2,501 of a manuscript; she scanned the page and realized that this was the book that Aksel was writing. Her heart pounding, she skimmed through the script.

DAILY NOTES TO BE FURTHER TRANSCRIBED:

"Today was a good day in ZONE XCV. The Hologram is morphing into a REAL woman/girl. I am molding Eve, slowly bending her to my Will. Not easy, she is fucking difficult. I see some advancement in her attitude. My studies of mind control are working. (Reread Edgar Pullenz's dissertation on My Mind Your Mind—in the box under the bed.) The Stockholm Syndrome is gospel. She is cooking me food and now her eyes have softened? when looking at me. I still don't know if this is reality or if my mind is playing tricks?? (am not taking my meds—don't need them) Will have to test. What I do know is that I will never let her go. I am Adam and she is Eve—mine for eternity. My feelings of anger and hate/love are still there. I will not forget the SUFFERING this BITCH put me through my entire life. **The SPROG remains the dilemma.** Do I keep or let it go? A mother cannot truly be a partner—her first allegiance is with her child. (My mother has never loved my father as much as she loves me.) This is a problem. More to follow."

Astrid jumped up from her seat and took Anja back to the sofa. She was shaking.

Aksel came into the room. He was topless and wearing gray sweatpants—pale, thin, with ribs showing through his transparent skin. He had shaved his head. In the dark, he was camouflaged, but in the light he was translucent.

"Rye bread and butter with coffee," he ordered.

Astrid got up and went to the kitchen. The bread was dense, dark, black, and grainy. It felt like cardboard in her hands. She smeared the butter on thick with a spreader.

"More butter," he said. "Who are you saving it for? And pickled herring."

"You may need to go to the grocery store," she said. "We are running out of food."

"Do you think that money grows on trees?" he said. "It does not. Unless you have a money tree like I do. My parents." He laughed hard.

"Your parents must be very worried about you. You should go and visit them."

"I bet your parents are worried about you more. You have disappeared off the face of the earth," he said.

"We should let them know that I am OK," she said. "Just to give them peace of mind."

"Calls can be traced, so that's not going to happen."

"Can I write a note and put it on their door?"

"I didn't realize how stupid you are," said Aksel.

Astrid poured Aksel another cup of coffee and brought it to the table.

"Aksel, please, I'm begging you. Our parents are not to blame for my behavior toward you. Your parents must be very concerned about your whereabouts."

"No, they are not. They think I am at a writing workshop. I always use that as an excuse to get away."

"Aksel, my parents have always been good to you. I just want to let them know that I am alive, that's it. Nothing more," Astrid said. "They will never know where I am, just that I am alive and with Anja."

"What's in it for me?" he asked. "Maybe if you were nicer to me?"

"I will cook you anything that you want, I will keep the place tidy, I will be more pleasant. You tell me and I will do it."

"Have you stopped bleeding?"

"No."

"Your mouth works, right?"

"I haven't had a dental cleaning in a long time," Astrid said. "I have gum disease."

"Yuck! You are such a turn-off," he said. "I almost feel sorry for your husband. I don't understand how you went for that spineless jellyfish. You both deserve each other."

Aksel was throwing and catching a rubber ball against the bare wall. The faster he spoke, the harder he hurled the ball until it hit a framed picture that came crashing down.

"For God's sake Astrid, your hands work," he yelled. "Go and wash your hands."

"I first want to make sure that you will let me contact my parents," she said.

"You just never let up, do you?" he said. "Nag, nag, nag."

Aksel went to his room, opened a drawer, and returned with a cell phone.

"This is what's called a burner phone. It can't be traced and it's not connected to anything."

"Can I call now? It's a good time because my parents would be home for lunch."

"You have to do the other thing first," he said. "Wash your hands, and to make double sure there are no crawlies, put on these disposable gloves." He threw them at her.

Astrid went to the bathroom and washed her hands.

"Put the baby out of the room," Aksel said. "I don't need her looking at me."

He came back with a towel and placed it on the sofa. He pulled down his sweatpants and kicked them on the floor. He then pulled down his Pikachu underpants.

"Put on the gloves," he ordered.

She pulled the rubber gloves over her hands. He handed her the tube of baby diaper cream.

"Turn off the lights," he said. "I'm ready."

He lay back. He looked like a mummy that Astrid had seen in a museum of Egyptian artifacts. Like one of the male servants who was buried with the Pharaoh. She then thought about what she would say when her mother picked up the phone. She would blurt out, "Mother it's me, I'm OK and Anja is with me." Her mother will be so relieved and happy.

"Don't be so rough," Aksel said. "Am I turning you on?"

Astrid wondered what her parents were eating. They had probably lost their appetites since she disappeared. If they knew that she and Anja were alive, they would eat again.

"Just stop," Aksel said. "I can't. If there ever was the opposite of sexy, that would be you."

He pulled up his pants, rolled up the towel, and threw it at Astrid.

"Can I call my parents?" she said.

"You didn't fulfill your part of the bargain," he said. "I could feel the hate in your hands."

"I tried my best. A promise is a promise. One thing I know, Aksel, is that you are a man of your word."

"I may not be a lot of things," he said, "but I mean what I say." He handed her the phone. Astrid dialed her house.

"*Hej*." It was her mother!

"Mother, it's me," Astrid said in a trembling voice.

"Who? Who is this?"

"Astrid."

Her mother gasped. "Astrid? Where are you? Are you OK? Jens! Jens! Come quickly."

Aksel stood beside her. "Few words," he mouthed.

"Mother, I want you to know that I am OK. I am with Anja; we both are OK."

"Where are you? When ..."

Aksel grabbed the phone away from her and turned it off.

"You owe me big time," he said.

Astrid was crying so hard that she couldn't speak. She fell to the ground sobbing.

"Enough!" he yelled. "They know you are alive. That's what you wanted, right? What they don't know is that you won't be coming back."

CHAPTER TWENTY-TWO

SARDINIA

Whenever Signora Melis felt depressed, the only remedy to lift her out of the fog was to go clothes shopping. She was very particular about the quality and fit. She only wore one hundred percent cotton or pure linen. She maintained that everything else made her sweat, and she was not having it.

Adela disagreed. "Cotton and linen crease too much. You always look rumpled in your clothes."

"I will never let polyester touch my body," she said.

Signora Melis's preferred dress shop was in a side street off the main square. Fashionista Boutique was the only place that she trusted for her outfits.

As she stepped in from the heat, the cool air perked her up like her favorite iced coffee. The bell rang to alert Signora Carolina that a customer had walked in.

She came rushing in from behind the counter, looking as though she had been interrupted from a nap. She blinked her eyes and puffed out her hair and flashed a big smile. Her teeth were covered in lipstick.

"*Buongiorno Signora*," she said, covering a yawn. "So good to see you. It's been too long."

"I've been so busy bottling tomatoes that I haven't had a minute."

"Can I help you find something?" Signora Carolina asked. She was an elegant woman, always dressed in the last season's styles from Milan. She confessed to Signora Melis that her budget only allowed her to buy things on sale.

"I'm looking for a dress."

"A dress with long sleeves? The weather is cooling down," Signora Carolina said. "I have some beautiful dresses that just came in. Perfect for you. Go into the changing room and I will bring an assortment through."

Signora Melis went into the little booth and shut the curtain behind her. She removed her dress and shoes. She was not happy with the woman looking back at her in the mirror. Since when did her stomach have a pouch? Her thighs looked dimpled and doughy. Her arms looked like the dry flowers she had pressed in a book as a hobby. Her face was yellow.

Signora Carolina came bounding toward her. "Signora, that's the old fitting room. Please follow me. I have remodeled new ones."

Signora Melis grabbed her things and was happy to exit the distorted house of mirrors. She was led into a newly renovated room with plush pink carpets and a gold tassel curtain.

She tried on the first dress that Signora Carolina hung up on the rail. She looked in the mirror. What an improvement! Her figure looked slimmer and firmer. She noticed a rosy glow on her skin. Pink light bulbs circled the mirror, and she wondered if that was the reason for the enhancement. The dress, however, was too boxy and fell below her knees.

"How is it?" called out Signora Carolina. "Step outside so I can have a look."

"I'm not sure about this one," said Signora Melis.

"I like it. It looks dignified," said Signora Carolina. "The green suits you."

"I look matronly," said Signora Melis. "I look like my mother."

"Elegant, not matronly," she said. "Try on the blue and gray patterned one."

Signora Melis pulled the green dress off over her head, then pulled the second dress on. It was a little tight and a bit of a struggle. She disliked trying on clothes; it was exhausting. She stepped out of the fitting room.

"*Perfetta!*" exclaimed Signora Carolina. "This dress is made for you."

Signora Melis kind of agreed. It was too tight, and it was too short, but she looked ... quite attractive, she thought.

"Can I have some water?" she asked. She was quite shocked at herself. "What am I thinking?" she thought.

She drank the glass of water fast. "I will take this," she said. Before Signora Carolina took the dress to the counter, she peeked at the price tag. It was much higher than she had wanted to spend but she decided that she deserved it.

Signora Melis opened her purse and took out her credit card.

"I'm happy that you found a pretty dress," said Signora Carolina. "I know that you have been through a very tough time."

"What makes you say that?" Signora Melis asked. "I haven't been through a tough time."

"I heard that your daughter and her husband had difficult circumstances regarding the birth of their baby girl."

Signora Melis swallowed, cleared her throat, and said, "What nonsense is that? Who would spread such rumors?"

Signora Carolina realized that she may have spoken out of turn. "I heard some story, probably lies." She fumbled, folding the dress into the bag, and the tissue paper tore.

"Who told you this?" Signora Melis said. "I insist that you tell me. Otherwise, I'm canceling the sale of this dress." She stood up straight and clenched her hands.

"Okay, okay, calm down Signora. You know that boy who runs around town thinking he is a big shot? Alessandro Cerutti? He told my daughter that the baby is not Adela's."

"What's all this commotion?" A disheveled man came out from the back of the store, his hair standing up like a rooster. He was shirtless. Signora Melis did not know who he was, but she did know that he was not Signora Carolina's husband.

Signora Melis was very quiet. She had a grim look of determination on her face. As she stepped out of the store with her shopping bag, Signora Carolina came running after her.

"Please don't tell anyone what I told you," she called out. But Signora Melis had already turned the corner.

She marched directly to Bar Sport. She knew exactly where to find Alessandro. She walked so fast that a puppy on the sidewalk yelped in fear and crouched to the side.

When she got to the bar, she saw Alessandro's motorbike parked outside. Signora Melis burst through the door. Alessandro was sitting at a table with a couple of men, smoking and watching soccer on the TV.

She strode up to him. "I heard you are spreading lies about my family," she said in his face. She clutched his hair, pulling his head back. The two men jumped up and moved out of the way.

"What are you talking about?" he answered, pinching his fingers together to emphasize his words. "Have you lost your mind?"

He pushed her off him, shoving her against the wall.

"Don't you ever mess with me or my family!" Signora Melis yelled.

He jumped up and ran out the door. "What are you going to do, old lady?" he shouted, mocking her voice. He leaped onto his bike, turned it on, and revved the engine loudly.

She raced after him and vaulted onto the back of his bike, burning her ankle on the exhaust pipe. She fell backward onto the street, reeling with pain. Alessandro reversed the bike, rode over her, and raced away.

Signora Melis lay in the street, not moving and bleeding. Everyone from the Bar rushed out to help her. "Don't move her, she is injured," someone said. Within minutes, the ambulance arrived, and the medics lifted her onto a gurney, put her in the ambulance, and drove to the hospital with sirens blaring.

Everyone knew who Signora Melis was. She was a prominent resident of Oristano. They knew her late husband, her family, and her circumstances, so they immediately called her daughter.

Signora Melis lay in the hospital bed. She had a broken rib and a fractured leg. Her head was bandaged where a deep gash was stitched. Adela, Luca, and Signor Rossi arrived soon after. They stormed past the nurse when she told them that she wasn't ready for visitors.

"Mama," cried Adela. "What did that bastard do to you?"

"We have to kill him," said Luca.

They had been told what had unfolded in the bar. Signor Rossi stood with his arms folded. "Justice will be served," he said. "We don't have to do anything. A worm finds his way out into the fire."

CHAPTER TWENTY-THREE

DENMARK

Gudrun was shaking so badly that she couldn't get the words out.

"Are you sure that was Astrid?" said Jens, stunned.

She nodded her head vigorously.

"How was her voice? Was it strong?"

"I don't know," she said, the words catching in her throat. "She sounded like herself."

"Was she traumatized?"

"Jens, how could I tell? Of course, she is traumatized. But with the grace of God, she called and said that she was OK. And that Anja is OK. They are together, that's all we want."

"Was there anything in the background? Did you hear the baby?" asked Jens. "Could she have been forced to say that they are OK and are together?"

"I don't know more. I know as much as you do, Jens. Call Officer Borgen immediately."

The detective's card was taped to the refrigerator. Jens called him right away and told him about the phone call from Astrid. Jens spoke in a calm and measured manner. Detective Borgen made him repeat the details a few times.

"We now know that mother and baby are together. That doesn't explain why they took the baby first and then the mother."

"Can you trace the call?" asked Jens.

"We are going to do all that we can. We need to get your cell phone. Can you please bring it into the office as soon as possible?"

"Of course."

"In the meantime, do not tell anyone about this phone call," said the detective before ending the call.

"Will they be able to tell where the call was coming from?" said Gudrun.

"They will do their best. That's what Officer Borgen said."

"I hope she and Anja are not hurt, I hope that they have food and shelter," said Gudrun. "Please God they aren't suffering. We haven't been able to eat or sleep since this happened. At least we now know that they are alive."

"Why would anyone take them? What is the reason?" Jens said. "It doesn't make sense."

Anton came into the living room. They gestured to him to come over.

"We heard from Astrid," Gudrun whispered. "She called my cell phone. She said that she and Anja are together and OK."

Anton felt his hands go numb. "Speak louder," he said. "Repeat what you said."

"We don't want Nanna to hear. She will tell everyone; the detective told us to keep this between us."

"Astrid sounded OK?" he said. "Did she sound like herself? She and our baby are alive?" He sat down and wept. "Thank you, God," he said. "I beg you to bring them back to us."

Gudrun sat on the back porch. This was her haven when she needed solace. It was not a large area, but her love of gardening had turned the outdoor space into her paradise. She had a love for flowers, particularly blooming bulbs; the bright colors always lifted her spirits. Purple and yellow tulips, golden daffodils, and pale blue crocuses in large ceramic pots flourished under her care.

But on this day, she was too distraught to appreciate their beauty. Gudrun only noticed that the brick flooring was chipped, and her favorite seagull ceramic wall hanging looked faded and worn. She was relieved to hear Astrid's voice, but at the same time, she feared for her daughter's and granddaughter's well-being. There were too many unanswered questions. Where were they? Did they have food? Were they abused? Who took them? Why? She didn't realize that she was crying loudly until Clara Sorensen seemed to magically appear and put her arms around her.

"It is very tough," said Clara, patting her on the back. "You have to have faith that they will come home soon."

"Promise me that you won't tell anyone?" said Gudrun.

"What is it?" said Clara. "Did something else happen?"

"We got a phone call yesterday evening. It was Astrid."

"Astrid? *Min Gud*! My God!"

"It was very quick. She said 'I am OK and Anja is OK. We are together.'"

"They are alive. Together. Thank God. Where? Did she sound normal?"

"That is all she said before she put the phone down."

"Will the police be able to trace the call?" said Clara.

"That is our hope."

"Has anyone asked for a ransom?" asked Clara. She stood up and was picking off the dead petals from the plants. She was deep in thought. "Who would want to kidnap them? If it's not for money, then what could be the reason?"

"Perhaps someone has a grudge against Astrid? A crazy person? A revenge thing?" said Gudrun, blowing her nose.

"The police must have asked all those questions. First Anja and then Astrid, who next?" Clara said. "Gudrun, we will do anything to help you. You are family to us. What hurts you, hurts us. Just know that."

Gudrun watched her neighbor and friend walk across the yard back home. She patted her hair down, blew her nose one last time, and went back indoors. Jens was sleeping in his armchair. He had become a fixture of a man struggling to function.

Nanna sat in the other chair staring into space. She didn't seem bored. She made up scenarios in her head and had conversations with imaginary people.

"What is the gloom and doom in this house?" shouted Nanna.

"Nanna, Astrid and the baby are still lost," said Gudrun.

"My little Gudrun, you have always been so dramatic. Astrid and that baby will be back, sooner or later. The sun still rises every day," Nanna said. "I am hungry, go and make me a sandwich."

CHAPTER TWENTY-FOUR

SARDINIA

The sun set late on a summer's night, so it was after nine o'clock and only turning to dusk when Luca and Adela sat outside Mama Sofia's eating dinner. Signora Melis had sent them out while she babysat Mira. She knew that the young couple had a lot to discuss. The air was still, and the only movement was the pigeons circling above, searching for a place to rest for the night. The barking of dogs echoed through the narrow, cobbled lane where they sat.

"What do you want to eat tonight?" asked Luca.

"I'm not hungry," said Adela. "I have no appetite."

"We are here, so you must have something, even something small."

"How can you think of eating when our lives are turned upside down?" Adela said.

"Life goes on," he said. "Things will settle down. You just have to have a better attitude."

"A better attitude? Are you kidding? You lied and you cheated. How will I ever trust you again?"

"We've been over this a thousand times, Adela, what do you want me to do? I was thinking only of you and how to make you happy."

"It would have been better if you had cheated with any other girl than Pia. That is a double betrayal," she said. "Luca, look at me, don't pretend that I'm not here." Adela tapped the table with the handle of her knife to get his full attention. "You always told me that you found Pia unattractive. You joked about her and said that she is overweight and gross. Did you say that to make me feel that nothing was going on between the two of you?"

"I don't find her attractive. I swear to you that I never looked at her sexually." He turned red and swallowed, realizing how foolish that sounded.

"When did this start? When I was pregnant? How terrible of you. You are the lowest of the low. Cheating on your pregnant wife."

"I was lonely. I felt that all you wanted from me was to father your child. You and your mother are a team, and I am an outsider."

"So, now you are blaming me? Is it my fault?" she said.

"It's not all your fault, but you never make me feel like you want me. We hadn't had sex for months. I have my needs too, you know."

"I was pregnant with our child, I didn't feel well. Sex was the last thing on my mind. You should have been more compassionate, not turning to someone else for your sexual needs." The longer Adela spoke, the angrier she became.

"There are two sides to a story," he said. "I asked Pia if she wanted to join me on the ride to Denmark. She wanted to get away from Alessandro, so she agreed. I parked the truck overnight at the truck stop, and one thing led to another."

"Stop. I don't want to hear anymore," said Adela, tearing up.

Mama Sophia approached them. She had a limp and she swayed from side to side as if wading through a vat of lard. One leg was shorter than the other, giving her a wobbly gait which was such a part of her that no one noticed it anymore.

"*Buona sera*," Mama Sophia said. "What brings you to eat at my table tonight?"

"We had to go out somewhere neutral to talk about our situation. We have been fighting nonstop," said Adela.

"That's always a good idea," she said. "You have to be polite in public. Eat well, have some wine, and everything will seem better. I have the perfect dish to comfort you—Pappardelle with ragu; it's so good, you will lick the plate."

"It will take more than a good plate of pasta to fix this marriage," said Adela.

"Sounds perfect to me," Luca interjected, pouring himself a glass of red wine from the carafe.

When Mama Sophia returned to the kitchen, Adela dialed her phone.

"*Ciao* Pia," she said. "Are you finished with work? Luca and I are at Mama Sophia's sitting outside; why don't you come and join us?"

Luca looked at Adela horrified. He mouthed, "Are you crazy?"

"No no, Pia, there won't be any shouting. We need to discuss things," said Adela, concluding the conversation.

Luca sat in silence, bouncing one leg up and down under the table. He poured another glass of wine.

Pia lived close by, so she arrived shortly, with her pink hair in disarray and out of breath. She kissed them both on both cheeks and lit a cigarette, blowing smoke in the air as she sat down.

"So, tell me," Adela said to Pia, "What's your excuse for sleeping with my husband? He tells me that he doesn't find you attractive. He was just lonely. What about you?"

"I'm sorry Adela. I didn't want to hurt you. I have no excuses."

"You ruined my life, Pia," she said.

"I hope I made up for it by giving you my baby," she answered.

"Don't say that," Luca said to Pia. "Your initial plan was to give her up for adoption. Only later did you decide that we were a better solution."

"That is the best solution for all of us. It worked out in the end for the best."

"She is *my* baby now," said Adela. "Not yours. You signed the papers."

Mama Sofia brought the bowls of pasta to the table; she placed them in front of Luca and Adela. She could feel the tension. She asked Pia what she would like to eat. Pia said she was not hungry.

"I don't want you near Mira anymore," said Adela. "You are not welcome in our home."

"That was the deal, Adela," Pia said, raising her voice. "You promised I could visit her. Luca, you promised too!"

"I don't want my baby near a whore and a slut!" Adela screamed.

"Calm down children," said Mama Sofia, pouring wine into their glasses. "*Mangia*, hunger always makes people angrier."

"Adela, stop screaming. Everyone is looking," Luca shushed.

"I don't care. Let everyone know that this piece of shit slept with my husband behind my back."

Adela got up from her seat, picked up her bowl of pasta, and dumped it over Pia's head. Pia jumped up with the pasta and sauce dripping from her head to her face.

"Bitch!" Pia shouted. "If your husband was happy with you, he never would have come to me."

Adela calmly turned around and said, "*Buona notte*, Mama Sofia. I apologize about your food, but it went to a good cause."

She left the restaurant and walked home in the dark.

CHAPTER TWENTY-FIVE

DENMARK

Astrid learned that in captivity the way of survival was to focus on the here and now. She did not allow herself to think about the future—it was too dark to go there.

She focused instead on minor details. Feeding Anja and taking care of her baby's needs; eating for survival even though she had no appetite. The most important factor was the most arduous task of not setting off the volatile nature of her captor, Aksel.

Astrid was aware that any talk of their past would fuel anger and resentment that he had kept bottled up inside of him for so many years. She had had no inkling of his feelings growing up. She recalled being kind and accepting of his weird behavior. Their classmates were always picking on him—his awkwardness and bizarre way of interacting with others. They teased him about his black clothes and red hair. They laughed at the way he spoke in short abrupt sentences, never making eye contact. Astrid took pity on him; after all, he was her neighbor and family friend, so she often stood up for him.

"Leave Aksel alone," she would say. "He is smarter than any of you put together."

"Why do you care about this creepy weirdo?" they would ask her.

"He is harmless," she would say. "Stop taunting him."

Aksel never knew that Astrid was on his side. She was popular and well-liked, so he presumed that she was just like all the others. It was true that she never accepted his offers to spend time alone with him. He had once asked her to go to the movies and she made an excuse.

Although Astrid didn't want to socialize with him, she made sure that she didn't hurt his feelings. She had invited him for bike rides to the park, but he refused her requests. It didn't make sense to her. He had asked her to dance at the school party and she pretended that she couldn't hear him above the music. Astrid never thought of that again, but Aksel never forgot it.

Astrid was sitting on the floor playing with Anja. She tried to normalize the situation so that Anja wouldn't know the difference. She sang to her and made funny faces to make her laugh. Anja would giggle and then let out a loud chuckle. It was at those moments that Astrid forgot for a brief moment where she was.

"Shut up," Aksel would say, bringing Astrid back to reality. "There is nothing that's funny."

Aksel had nothing to do all day except pretend that he was busy. He was on his laptop staring at the screen for hours. He waited for Astrid to prepare him meals, and although he never complimented the food, he ate it with gusto.

Aksel only left the cabin to shop for food and groceries. He made sure to lock and bolt every window and door. For the remainder of the time, he slept. He slept a lot, but even in sleep, he was restless. He would shout and scream, lashing out so physically that at times he fell off the bed. Astrid tried hard not to allow her baby to disturb him because when she cried, he would blow up and scream for hours.

"Keep her quiet or I will quiet her forever," he said.

Anja felt an icy cold sweep over her.

"I am trying," she said, rocking Anja. "Babies sometimes cry for no reason."

"Do you remember your orange kitten?"

"Yes," said Astrid.

"You called her Comet, and I called her Vomit."

"She went missing. I looked all over for her. I was heartbroken."

"She didn't go missing. She was always meowing day and night. I twisted her head off and threw her in the lake," he said, looking pleased with himself.

"Oh my God," said Astrid.

"Why are you so shocked? It was just a cat."

His phone rang.

"Fuck, it's my mother," he said. "Keep quiet. Keep that sprog quiet."

"Hello," he said, walking to his bedroom. He didn't close the door.

"I am fine," he said. "The workshop is winding down. What? I don't use a credit card. You know that Mother. Only cash. I've told you a thousand times, I don't trust credit cards; anyone can take your information and use it. Oh, come on. *Det er skort*, that is crazy. You are not transferring cash anymore? Is this father's idea? My therapist? Fuck him. You are not enabling me. How can you cut off your child? You are a terrible parent. Do you want to see me starve? Is that what you want?"

Aksel was pacing up and down, running his hand through his hair and pulling at it. He noticed that Astrid was listening. He shot her a furious look and banged the door shut.

"I will have to kill myself!" he screamed at his mother. "Is that what you want?"

He ended the conversation. Astrid could hear him mumbling to himself. He burst through the door.

"How much money do you have on you?" he asked Astrid.

"A few hundred kroner."

"That's it?"

"I didn't come prepared, Aksel. Remember?"

"I have to get some money, or we won't eat," he said. "At least you won't eat. I will always find a way."

"I have an idea," said Astrid.

"What? Go rob a bank?"

"How about you ask for ransom for the return of me and Anja?"

He swung his head toward her, squinting his eyes and pursing his lips.

"Not bad for an idiot. The only thing is that I'm not letting you go for any amount of money. That's a certain way for them to find me."

"Not if you are clever. You can arrange for a pickup and not deliver the goods. Kidnappers do that all the time," she said.

"You have been watching too much crime TV," he said. "Cameras are all over, it's a sure way of being caught. Do you think that I'm so stupid?"

Astrid didn't say anything anymore, but she could tell that he was thinking this through. He sat at the kitchen counter strumming his fingers as if playing the piano, his nails clicking frantically on the wood.

"What do you want for lunch?" she asked.

"That's all you think about is food?"

"There are some cold cuts in the fridge. I can make you a salami sandwich on rye."

"Such a good *housewifey* you are," he said in a high-pitched mocking voice.

"We still have enough food for a few days," Astrid said. "Then you can come up with a plan. You are good at that."

"Don't talk crap," he said. "The best plan would be if you went and earned your keep on the street. If you know what I mean. But we would starve. No man would pick up a shrew like you. Even if you gave it away for nothing."

CHAPTER TWENTY-SIX

SARDINIA

It wasn't easy for Signora Melis to walk on crutches. She was used to an active lifestyle. She was losing her patience to heal. She couldn't clean or go food shopping, and she found it difficult to balance and cook at the same time. The only thing that she insisted on was going to Mass every day. She hobbled along the familiar path, and even though it took her longer, she went. Mass was a balm for her soul, and she could not live a day without it. She would have crawled to get there.

"Signora, what has happened to you?" asked the Padre as she shuffled into the cathedral.

"There are not enough hours in the day to tell you what I have been through," she answered.

"Come into my office," he said. "You can give me the short version."

Signora Melis followed the Padre into his office. There were mounds of papers and files stacked up on every surface, including the desk. The shelves were lined with leather-bound books and more files reaching to the high-domed ceiling. Even with all these yellowed papers, the office was cluttered but not messy. The Padre and his assistant knew where every item was. They refused to use the computer, so it still lay in its box on the floor, and the congregants did not complain. If someone needed a copy of their great-grandmother's christening certificate, it was found.

"Sister Luisa, can you please bring Signora Melis a cup of tea?" asked the Padre.

"Please tell me your story," he said to Signora Melis.

She left her tea untouched, took a deep breath, and said, "Padre, if you fall asleep, I will forgive you."

He smiled. "It is nearly time for my siesta, Signora, so if I snore, please forgive me."

"Adela lost a baby boy at the beginning of the year. A few weeks later, Luca arrived back from a work trip with a newborn baby girl. He told us that he found her abandoned in the park. We were shocked and dubious, but we accepted this as God's will and took the baby into our hearts and home. Luca gave Adela small hints that this baby was found in a foreign country. Adela, Luca, and I treated the baby as if she was born to us. We felt guilty in one way because we knew that she was a missing child but because we were told that she was abandoned by her birth mother, we reconciled that she wasn't wanted.

"Then everything came crashing down. One afternoon, AISE, the External Intelligence Agency, visited us. They had information that the baby did not belong to us. There was a tragic event in Copenhagen, Denmark. It was all over the media there. A baby girl was kidnapped from her carriage outside a restaurant. The detectives deduced that our baby, who we call Mira because she is a miracle, was that same missing baby. They took DNA samples from Adela and Luca. After a week, the results came back. It was a big shock. Adela, as we already knew, was not the biological mother, but it turned out that Luca is the biological father!"

"*Dio mio*," said the Padre, sitting up in his chair, wide awake. "Please continue."

"It turns out that Luca and this girl Pia, who was Adela's best friend, were cheating and Pia fell pregnant."

Is this Pia Lanconi, the orphan?" the Padre asked.

"Yes."

"She grew up in your house. I baptized her."

"Yes. That is her. That's the thanks I get for taking her in. So, she is pregnant, and they hear of this abduction story in Denmark. Luca was going back and forth in his truck making deliveries to Denmark. They hatched a plan. Pia did not want an abortion, thank the Lord, so she offered to give up the baby to Adela and Luca to raise as their own. They both knew that Adela would never agree to a child born from an affair of her husband's. They decided to make it look like they kidnapped a baby from Denmark."

"That was a crazy plan," the Padre said, "but better than abortion."

"It's also better than stealing someone else's child," said Signora Melis. "It's a mess, as you can imagine." She tapped the desk as if playing the piano. "Pia signed the papers to relinquish all parental rights."

"Has the baby been found in Denmark?" asked the Padre.

"I don't think so. We haven't seen any more news." Signora Melis took a sip of her tea, her throat dry from talking.

"Dear Signora, you haven't told me why you are injured and using crutches," said the Padre.

"That's the result of trying to defend my family's honor. Alessandro Cerutti has caused great harm to our reputation through his lies and evil ways. I confronted him and he drove over me with his motorbike."

"God will punish the sinners. You don't have to take matters into your own hands. Trust in the Lord and He will protect you," said the Padre.

"The thing is that this has damaged Adela and Luca's marriage," Signora Melis said. She looked up and saw that the Padre had fallen asleep with his head on his chest. She let herself out and hopped home on her crutches.

When she came home, Signor Rossi was mopping the marble floors. He had been very helpful since she was injured by the motorbike.

"Where were you?" he asked. "I was worried."

"I went to the church," she said. "Thank you so much for helping me around the house."

"It's nothing," he said. "Can you smell something nice from the kitchen?"

"I can. Is that chicken cacciatore? It smells delicious. The chicken, garlic, mushrooms, and wine give it away."

"I used the first jar of our canned tomatoes; I think they are the best we've made." After he finished mopping the floors, he went to the kitchen to stir the chicken in the pot on the stove.

Signora Melis was always impressed by how domesticated Signor Rossi was. Her late husband had no interest in cooking or running the house. Most of the men her age did not help their wives at home. With the older generation, that was the way it was. The women did the housework, the men went to work. Things had changed for the better now. She admired Signor Rossi for thinking like a modern man.

He helped her sit at the table. He poured her a glass of water, placed a napkin on her lap, and dished out the chicken with a side of rice, placing the plate in front of her. She felt like a queen.

Signor Rossi sat down, put his napkin under his chin, and before he took a bite, he looked up at Signora Melis. He poured a glass of red wine and passed it to her. He poured a glass of wine for himself and lifted his glass.

"I want to make a toast, Signora," he said in a firm voice. "May all your troubles be over. We ask the Lord for good health and quick healing for you. Both physically and mentally." He reached forward to clink their glasses. "*Salute*!" he bellowed.

"*Salute*!" Signora concurred.

"Signora, I must confess that lately I have been looking at you with different eyes."

Signora Melis spluttered and coughed, choking on her wine.

"I didn't mean to scare you, Signora," he said.

"Salvatore, you can call me Rosalia. Signora is too formal for our lengthy relationship. We have known each other long enough to be on first-name terms."

"I appreciate that, Signora."

"Rosalia," she corrected.

"Yes, yes, Rosalia."

"Salvatore. That too sounds so strange to me," Rosalia said, blushing.

They both laughed and ate their food as if nothing had happened. But it had. When Signor Rossi stood up to remove Signora Melis's plate, their hands touched for longer than needed. She smiled to herself as she listened to him sing his favorite Italian ballads while washing the dishes.

CHAPTER TWENTY-SEVEN

DENMARK

"How much do you think that you are worth?" Aksel asked, jumping up behind Astrid as she sat reading. He now allowed her to read the books in the cabin.

She jumped. "You gave me such a fright," she said. "What do you mean?"

"For your ransom. Maybe it's not such a bad idea after all."

"It's not how much I'm worth, it's how much my parents can afford to pay."

"Two million kroner?" he asked. "That's not a lot of money for your child and grandchild. Unless they don't even want you back."

Astrid tried to keep her voice steady and controlled. "My parents are not wealthy. You would need them to have ready cash in hand."

Aksel was never still when he wasn't asleep. He was throwing a ball into a net attached to the bedroom door. "There will be no police involved," he said, aiming the ball and missing the net. "I repeat, no authority involvement."

"Of course," she said. "We need this to work. I don't want my baby to starve, or me either. We have to have food and supplies."

"I'm warning you now, if anything goes wrong with this plan, meaning if the police are involved, I will kill your parents." He got a slam dunk. "Yes!" he shouted in glee.

"I understand," she said. "I am very aware of the consequences."

"I'm sure you are thinking all kidnappers say the same thing. But I mean it. I am not afraid of doing anything. Even to you. I don't care if I have to go down in a gunfight. My life isn't worth living anyway."

"I give you my word. I believe you," she said.

"It's two million kroner," Aksel said. "It's not worth the hassle for less."

He went to the refrigerator and took out a beer. "Want one?" he asked.

"No, thank you."

"You are a graphic designer so I need your expertise to write a ransom note that no one can trace."

"Anything on a computer can be traced," Astrid said. "The tried-and-true way is to cut out letters from a magazine and write the note using them."

"That's so dated," he said. He spoke rapidly, enjoying putting the plan in motion.

"Dated doesn't matter. It's what works that is important. I just want to feed Anja and then we can get to work. We will need magazines, glue, and some scissors."

"It's always all about the baby," he said.

"Don't forget I am worth more with the baby. Keep that in mind."

Astrid tried not to tremble. She was pleased that Anja could hold the bottle herself because she did not trust her hands from shaking. She hoped that this would work as she planned. The authorities, her parents, or someone out there would foil this and be able to find them. This was her only chance for freedom.

Astrid's hope of DNA matching was dashed when she saw that Aksel was wearing disposable gloves. He had meticulously wiped down the table before placing magazines on top.

"What should I write?" he asked Astrid.

"Something like: I HAVE YOUR DAUGHTER AND GRANDDAUGHTER. 2 MILLION DANISH KRONER IS REQUESTED FOR THEIR SAFE RELEASE. DO NOT INVOLVE THE AUTHORITIES OR THERE WILL BE DIRE CONSEQUENCES AND YOU WILL NEVER SEE THEM AGAIN.

YOUR DAUGHTER WILL CALL YOUR HOME NUMBER ON A NON-TRACEABLE PHONE TO GIVE INSTRUCTIONS WHERE TO DROP THE CASH. WHEN THE MONEY IS IN ORDER

YOUR DAUGHTER AND CHILD WILL BE IMMEDIATELY RELEASED."

"That is too long," said Aksel. "Too many letters to cut out. Use the first paragraph and then add 'Your daughter will call you.' You have to call so they know that you are alive. Also, change the word "I" have your daughter to "We" have your daughter."

"If you get the money, why won't you let me and Anja go?"

He laughed maniacally. "Because, dummy, you will immediately tell them who took you."

"What if I promise that I won't?" Astrid pleaded. "It would be a win-win for both of us."

"I don't only want the money. I need to keep you, idiot. But you are so high maintenance, you and that baby are bankrupting me."

"You could use the money and live a good life somewhere else. We are holding you back. It would be a win-win situation for both of us," Astrid said.

"I can't believe that you think I am that gullible and stupid," he seethed. "You insult my intelligence." He marched up to Astrid and slapped her hard in the face.

Astrid recoiled, holding her throbbing cheek in shock, but would not let him see the tears welling in her eyes.

"Look what you made me do!" He yelled so loudly that Anja started crying from fear. "I have treated you so well and this is the thanks that I get?" He put his face close to hers and shouted, "Say sorry or I will have to hit you again!"

"Sorry."

"Say, 'Sorry Aksel. Please forgive me.'"

"Sorry, Aksel. Forgive me."

"*Please* forgive me. Where are your manners?" he yelled.

"Please forgive me."

"Now make up that damn letter and shut your mouth," he said.

Astrid sat at the table. Her cheeks were stinging, and she could hardly see through her tears. She tore out pages from the old magazines and started cutting out letters. She pasted them with a glue stick onto the white paper. It looked exactly how she had seen ransom notes in the movies done this way. She knew there was no way of putting a secret message in the note because Aksel was too observant.

When she was finished, she left the message on the table and went to lie down on her bed with Anja. She could hear Aksel in the dining room.

"That looks OK," he called out. "How do you propose we get it to your parents?"

"Make your own plans," she mumbled.

He came into her room. The door had been removed so he could see and hear her at all times.

"What did you say?" he asked. "What do we do next?"

"Tack the note on my parent's front door," she said. "They go in and out all day."

"Is the mailbox not a better idea?"

"They don't always get the mail immediately, so it may hinder the plan," she said nonchalantly as if discussing an everyday event.

"That's true," he said. "I will go after midnight when everyone is asleep and tack this on the door. Get up off the bed, don't be so lazy. It's lunchtime and I'm hungry."

Astrid got up, sighing. "Do you want pickled herring and cucumber salad?"

"If that's all you can come up with," Aksel said. "You are lucky that I am so easy to please."

They sat down to eat. Astrid didn't touch her plate.

"You are not eating?" he said.

"I'm not hungry."

"You should eat something. You are wasting away. It's not attractive to look like a skeleton."

"Can I be excused?" Astrid said. "I need to go to the bathroom."

"Again?"

"I have to pee."

"You have peed a hundred times today."

"I have a bladder infection."

"Jesus, Astrid. What the hell? Everything is wrong with you. I wish I had known this before."

"You mean you wouldn't have kidnapped me?"

"I didn't think it through. Remember I took the baby first, then you. I didn't know that I was getting a hypochondriac."

"Are you sorry?"

"Nope. I am enjoying our little family. I'm banking on you falling for me soon. Then we can have a real relationship."

When Astrid came back to the table, Anja was in her arms. She was a happy baby, always smiling. This was the only thing that gave Astrid a sense of purpose and the will to go on.

Aksel had finished eating and was ready to discuss the rest of the plan. Once Astrid's parents read the ransom note, Astrid was to call them and give them instructions on where to drop the money. Once the money was checked by Aksel, who would be waiting in the shadows covered from head to toe in black, they were going to expect Astrid and Anja to be released. That was not happening. He would have the money and they could continue to hide out and be together.

"Aren't your parents going to look for you?" asked Astrid.

"My parents will make a show of looking for me, but they will be relieved when they can't find me. I was always a thorn in their side."

* * *

"Jens! Jens! Come here," called Gudrun.

Jens came running to the front door where his wife was standing, looking as if she had seen a ghost.

"What Gudrun? What's the matter?"

"Look. There is a note stuck on our door. I went out to get the newspaper and found this."

There was the note that Aksel had pinned on the door in the middle of the night.

Jens reached out to take it down.

"Don't touch it," Gudrun ordered. "There may be fingerprints. Get your gardening gloves."

Jens came back with rubber gloves on and carefully removed the note. They immediately took it inside and shut the door.

They both read the pasted letters and stood with their mouths open, not knowing what to do.

"We will get the money immediately," said Gudrun. "We have to do whatever they say. We have to get Astrid and Anja back. No matter what."

"This was all about money, but that's OK. As long as our children are safe and cared for."

"Don't tell anyone," Jens whispered. "This is a very delicate situation."

They read the note over and over, shaking so much that they couldn't hold the page still.

"All we want is Astrid and her baby back home." Gudrun looked at her husband and said slowly and clearly, "We must not involve the police."

"Do you think that is the right thing to do?" he asked.

"Absolutely. I don't want anything to go wrong. The police can ruin it for us."

"We will do exactly what they say," said Jens. "Even though this is not the right thing to do, we don't want to jeopardize anything."

"The letter says that Astrid will phone us. We don't know which phone—the home line or our cell phones. We must keep all three open and wait."

"Can't the police trace the call?"

"I don't know. I'm sure the kidnappers are aware of that," said Jens.

They didn't know what to do with themselves. They were too anxious to sit or to stand, so they paced the floor instead.

Jens suddenly realized the reality of the situation. "I don't think that we have two million krone cash available. What are we to do?" Then, to calm himself down he said, "Everything is under control. I will find a way."

"How much do we have?" asked Gudrun. "I have savings that I can liquidate in my account."

"Me too. But it's not enough. We have to get on this immediately."

Gudrun started breathing heavily and banging on her chest.

"Stop," commanded her husband. "Do not allow yourself to panic. We have to think clearly."

Jens was a man who was used to coming up with a plan. He lived by the motto—*there are no problems, only solutions.* Before retirement, he was a top manager in the headquarters of the Copenhagen Bus Transportation Systems so he was used to putting out fires. The memorable year, when the bus drivers went on strike, was resolved solely due to his expertise in negotiation. The drivers were seeking an increase in salaries, and it was Jens who was able to get them back behind the wheel, not for the raise they were seeking but close enough. The transportation company was impressed with Jens's capability and awarded him an honorary plaque for his office wall. So, when he stood silently contemplating how to come up with the money for the kidnappers, it wasn't long before he had a plan.

"Dr. Sorensen," he announced to Gudrun. "The Sorensens. They will help us."

"How?" she asked.

"With the money. They may have the available funds and we can ask them for a loan," said Jens.

"I don't want to involve them," cried Gudrun. "I don't want to burden them with our problems."

"We have no option. They are our closest friends."

The shrill ringing of the house phone shocked them out of their thoughts.

"It could be the call," she mouthed to her husband as if the room was bugged.

He leaped across the room to pick up the phone.

"Hello," he said, motioning for Gudrun to listen in.

"*Far,* father," Astrid's voice was soft but clear.

"Astrid, my darling, are you OK?" said Jens, holding back his tears.

"Yes. We are fine. If you want to see us again, you have to follow these directions. Don't talk, just listen. Do not, I repeat, do not call the police. If you do, then you will never see us again. You must bring the money tomorrow night in a plastic shopping bag. Do you know the lane off Lager Straede where we drop off our garbage?"

"Yes."

"Place the bag in the garbage bin tomorrow night at exactly 9:00 p.m. Step back into that doorway and turn to face the door. Do not peek. Someone will be there to count the money. If it is correct, then Anja and I will be let free from across the lane."

Jens heard her cover the handpiece and heard muffled voices.

"Hello?" he said.

"I'm here. Please, Father, don't alert the authorities. You want us back, right?"

"Yes. I will not call the police."

"Promise?"

"You have my word."

Astrid put down the phone.

Jens and Gudrun fell into each other's arms crying. They rocked back and forth.

"All we want is for Astrid and the baby to come home safe to us," sobbed Gudrun.

"The money means nothing to us. We just want them back," cried Jens.

The Nielsens made a pact to do exactly what their daughter had asked. Jens blew his nose, washed his face, put on his cap, and went next door.

He knocked gently.

"Good evening neighbor," said Dr. Sorensen. "Good to see you. Come inside."

"Who is there?" called Clara from the bedroom.

"A surprise guest! Neighbor Jens."

Clara came rushing out to greet him in her nightgown and slippers. "Welcome, welcome," she said.

They noticed immediately that Jens looked stricken and serious.

"Have you heard anything about Astrid and Anja?" asked Clara.

"Can we sit down for a minute?" said Jens. "I have to ask you a personal favor."

Dr. Sorensen pulled up a chair at the dining room table and gestured for him to join. The three of them sat upright waiting for Jens to finish blowing his nose and start talking.

"I need cash immediately," he said. "A serious sum. Two million krone."

"Yes," said Dr. Sorensen.

"I have about half, and I need the other half," Jens said.

"When do you need it?" asked Dr. Sorensen, twisting his mustache.

"Tomorrow morning. As soon as possible."

"We will have it for you by tomorrow morning," said Dr. Sorensen.

"We will help you with whatever you need," said Clara.

Jens stood up. "Thank you," he said.

He put his cap back on, exhaled, and walked out the door.

* * *

The weather was clear and mild on the drop-off day. Aksel was in a jolly mood. He whistled in the shower, something Astrid had never heard before. It was as if he was looking forward to the big event. He had gone grocery shopping in the nearby village and spent most of the remaining money in anticipation of the upcoming windfall.

He even bought a bottle of champagne and put it in the refrigerator to chill.

"What are we celebrating?" asked Astrid.

"I'm celebrating that finally you are paying for your keep."

"Just to confirm. You are going to go and pick up the money, then leave my parents standing there waiting for me and Anja's return?"

"Yup. That's the plan."

"How long do you think that two million kroner will last you under these circumstances? In a year or two would you be planning another heist?"

"Why are you such a pessimist? Can't you look on the bright side? Be happy for once," he said. "I will cross that bridge when I come to it."

"Are we going to remain here when you go pick up the money?" said Astrid.

"Do you want to come with me on the drive?" he asked her as if they were going to get ice cream.

"And Anja?"

"She can stay here. I left her many times on her own and she was fine."

Astrid shook her head. She could imagine how devastated her parents would be when they realized that she and Anja were not released. She couldn't bear to think of their disappointment. Aksel had warned her that if the plan went awry, he would burn down her parents' house. When she argued that his parents' house would likely go down in the fire too, his answer was, so be it.

After a leisurely dinner, Aksel dressed in a black hoodie and black jeans and put a black ski mask in his pocket to cover his face. He also packed a gun. He wore black rubber gloves. He took a black backpack to bring home the money.

Aksel decided that he would go into the city by train instead of driving. "No one will suspect me on a train," he said. "It will be a quick in and out." He also made sure to lock and bolt any escape possibility and took his burner cell phone.

Before he left, he blew Astrid a kiss. "Wish me luck," he said as he stepped out into the night.

Aksel took the train and arrived in the city at 8:45 p.m. He put on the ski mask that covered his whole face except for his eyes and walked briskly to the assigned place. He didn't run to avoid detection. When he reached the lane, he stood behind a wall where he could see the assigned trash can. At exactly 9:00 p.m., he saw Jens open the trash can lid and place a bag inside. He then stepped away and, as instructed, faced the wall. He was alone.

Just as Aksel was creeping toward the can, he heard the sound of rustling leaves coming from the opposite side. He stopped in his tracks and hid behind a parked car. He heard whispers and footsteps. It was a group of policemen with guns drawn. Before they even proceeded out of the bushes, Aksel had turned and made his escape.

With bright lights glaring, the police approached Jens, who was still standing facing the wall.

He turned abruptly and started screaming, "What are you doing? Why are you here?"

They grabbed him and walked him to an unmarked police car. "You are in danger. Get in the car."

"You have ruined it! My daughter, my baby, they were coming back." He put his face in his hands and sobbed in the back of the police car.

"We have to protect you. There is a team of men with search dogs scouring the area. We will get them," an officer explained.

"We didn't want you," shouted Jens. "You have ruined the plan."

"We had to protect you and catch the bastards and find your children," said the officer.

"How did you know about this?" Jens cried.

"We have recorders on your phones. We have to know at all times."

"You ruined the plan," Jens whispered in despair. "How will I tell my wife?"

Aksel kicked in the door when he arrived back at the cabin. He threw his backpack at the wall and kicked the table until it broke. He then punched his bedroom door until there was a huge hole.

Astrid crouched with Anja, facing the corner of the room. She realized that something had gone terribly wrong. All she could think about was the safety of her parents. The crazier Aksel got, the more she cowered speechlessly. Until he started kicking her.

As he kicked her back, he ranted, "The fucking police were there!"

She pulled Anja into her chest and wrapped her body around her while Aksel continued to kick her. He finally stopped and crashed on the sofa.

"Your fucking parents called the police," he said. "How did I trust them? I should have known from the beginning."

Astrid sat curled on the floor until she heard him go to his room and slam the door shut. Anja had remained silent the entire time as if she sensed that they were in danger.

CHAPTER TWENTY-EIGHT

SARDINIA

"Signora," Signor Rossi called out to Signora Melis as she was hanging up the washing on the line.

"Rosalia," she reminded him.

"*Si*, Rosalia. Would you like to take a walk with me to the promenade for some ice cream?"

"That would be lovely. It's a nice cool day for a walk. Let me finish hanging the laundry and we can go. Do you think it may rain today?"

"I don't think so. There isn't a cloud in the sky."

Signora Melis hurried up with her daily chores. She was going to bake sourdough bread, but she felt that going with Signor Rossi down to the sea was a welcome break in her routine. She went inside, changed into a pink linen dress, brushed her hair, and put on some pink lipstick. Adela would approve. She found Signor Rossi waiting for her on the front porch. He looked quite spritely in a navy blazer, cream pants, and brown leather loafers.

"Signora, I mean Rosalia, you look very pretty. Pink suits you," he said, looking her up and down.

Signora Melis wasn't used to compliments, especially from a man, so she looked at the ground awkwardly.

"Salvatore, you look quite attractive yourself," she said, staring at his shoes.

The walk to the promenade was a familiar route for them. The cobbled sidewalks were smooth and polished from centuries of use. They passed the arched gray stone buildings where they shopped for as long as they could remember. Senora Melis could do all her daily shopping on Via Antico. The butcher, the fruit vendor, the bakery, the hairdresser, clothes stores, coffee shops, and restaurants. She crossed over the street to the pharmacy, the cobbler, and the Tabacchi that her husband had owned. She and Signor Rossi spoke very little on their brisk walk, mainly one-word answers.

"Are you comfortable?" asked Signor Rossi.

"Yes," she replied.

"Are you too warm?"

"No."

Along the way they were greeted by townspeople, some they knew well, others they were not as familiar with. But there was no one that they didn't know at all.

People called out, "*Buongiorno!*" and they repeated the salutations.

There were always a few busybodies who did a double take seeing the Signora and Signore together. This was not a common sight, and the event would bring many hours of speculative conversation.

They arrived at their destination. The boardwalk was where Adela and Luca's wedding took place some time ago. It was a long, wide footpath that bordered the white sand and turquoise water. Chunky palm trees lined the path, spilling their shade over the interspersed benches that were always filled with people staring into space. *Dolce far niente,* the sweetness of doing nothing. Just being in the present—contemplating life. The peaceful view of the ocean lulled each one into a meditative state. It was the vendor of the ice cream stall's persistent calling that jolted everyone awake.

"Come buy this delicious ice cream!" he announced. "The best in the entire world!" Mounds of colorful flavors made it impossible to choose only one. The overflowing scoops of *gelato* pressed into the sugar cones started melting before the first lick.

Signora Melis chose the strawberry flavor, and soon it was dripping down her wrist.

"Oh dear," she said. "I'm a messy ice cream eater."

Signor Rossi had a brown mustache from the chocolate flavor.

"Excuse me, Rosalia, this is not a good look." They both laughed.

A tender camaraderie enveloped them as they sat quietly eating their ice cream on the bench. There were no racing heartbeats or ticklish feelings; just a comforting warmth, like stepping into a warm bath.

Signor Rossi held Signora Melis's chin in his hand and gently wiped the ice cream off her mouth with a paper napkin.

"Rosalia," he said, seriously looking into her eyes. "I would like to further our relationship into something more solid. How do you feel about that?"

She licked the remainder of the ice cream off her wrist and answered, "I am agreeable to your proposition."

"That makes me very happy," he said. "How do you propose we should proceed?"

"There cannot be any physical interaction between us because it won't look proper in the eyes of others," she answered. "Especially for my parents in heaven and my late husband."

"That is true," he said, contemplating their situation. "I have a solution," he added. "We should get married to do this correctly in the eyes of the church."

"I agree," she said, nodding her head. "That makes sense."

"Well then, that's the plan!" he said joyfully, squeezing her hand. "We will tell our children that we plan to be married in two weeks."

"Why so fast?" said Senora Melis.

"Because I can't wait that long to kiss you."

They held hands the whole way back home, which must have given many people things to talk about, but they did not care. They knew that they had a plan in place.

When they walked through the front door, they could tell that Adela was not happy. Her face was flushed, her eyes swollen from crying, and her lips pressed tightly together.

"Is something wrong?" asked Signora Melis.

"You are not going to believe this," she said. "Pia and Alessandro are engaged."

"I thought she hated him," said Signor Rossi. "He has caused her such grief."

"She must have changed her mind," said Adela. "She came around to tell me her 'good' news."

"Wasn't he indicted for forgery? What about my case against him? He nearly killed me on his motorbike. I am waiting for information from the police," said Signora Melis.

"Pia told me that there wasn't enough evidence for the forgery and there wasn't any evidence for your assault."

"Someone must have paid off the judges," said Signor Rossi. "That goes on all the time."

Mira toddled up to Signora Melis, raising her arms to be lifted.

"Come my sweetheart. Nonna loves you." Mira buried her head in Signora Melis's shoulder.

"I cannot understand Pia," Adela said. "She knows Alessandro's true colors, so why would she want to marry such a bad person? I have lost all my respect for that girl. They deserve each other."

"Cut her out of your life," said Signora Melis.

"They are going back to Bari, to his family," said Adela. "That will be a good thing."

Signora Melis put Mira down and took out the dishes from the cabinet to set the table for dinner. Signor Rossi immediately jumped up to help. He glanced at her and gave her a wink. They felt joyful at their decision for a future together, but this was not the right time to tell the family.

The ritual of setting the table for meals gave Signora Melis a sense of comfort and security. As she placed the blue-and-white dishes and cutlery in each place setting in the same order day after day, she felt at peace. The table was usually set for four but often there were more. She felt sad that for so many years Pia had a permanent seat at the table. But life was like that. She had learned to adapt. Adela had told her that she, Luca, and the baby would be moving out into their place soon. They needed privacy, and Mira needed a room of her own. Signora Melis was pleased that they had decided to give their marriage a second chance.

CHAPTER TWENTY-NINE

DENMARK

Anja was crying. Her little face scrunched up, bright red, her mouth forming a perfect circle emitting distressed howls. Now that she realized her cries would be answered, she cried like a normal baby.

"Make her stop!" Aksel yelled, covering his ears with his hands. "I'm trying to watch my TV show." He always watched true crime stories, giving his opinions on how the criminals were so stupid to be caught. Aksel was very distressed that the ransom scheme that he had believed was foolproof had backfired.

His erratic moods had accelerated after that incident, so when he complained about the baby crying, Astrid jumped up, alarmed at his harsh tone.

"Since you've been here, she hasn't stopped crying. It's getting on my nerves," he said, thumping the table so hard that the cups and saucers jiggled up and down. “She was better behaved without you.”

Astrid picked Anja up and rocked her back and forth, trying to calm her, but she cried even louder. Astrid hummed a lullaby that usually quietened her, but it did not work. She put the bottle in her mouth, hoping that the warm milk would do the trick, but Anja screamed louder.

Aksel stormed toward Astrid, pushed her aside, and grabbed Anja out of her arms.

“I said shut up!” he hollered, roughly shaking her up and down.

“Stop! Stop!” Astrid screamed, reaching up to pull Anja away from him.

He lifted her beyond Astrid’s reach and shook her harder, back and forth like a rag doll.

Astrid threw herself at him, kicking him as hard as she could on his shins. “*Fuck dig!* Fuck you!” he shouted, dropping Anja on the floor. She lay limp on the carpet, silent, with her eyes shut. Astrid panicked, scooping her up to her chest and running her hands all over her little body feeling for damage.

“What have you done to my baby?” she screamed.

Astrid rushed to the kitchen sink and put Anja’s head under the cold running water, letting the water stream over her hair. Anja opened her eyes, whimpering.

“We have to take her to the hospital,” Astrid said, frantically wrapping a towel around Anja. “Get the van right now,” she ordered.

"No," said Aksel, with his arms folded across his chest.

"Now!" she begged. "Please, please, or she will die."

"And why would I care?" he said, shrugging.

"You are a terrible person," Astrid cried, "but you are not a murderer. Let's go now."

Aksel looked at his reflection in the full-length mirror on the door, turning his head from side to side. He pursed his lips as if he was about to whistle, admiring his profile. He patted down his hair, flicking his bangs out of his eyes.

"Please, Aksel, let's go." Astrid said as she cradled Anja in her arms, blowing lightly on her face.

Aksel pushed up his sleeves and flexed, posing to the left, then to the right.

"Do you find me attractive?" he said. "Sexy?"

"Aksel!" she screamed. "If anything happens to Anja, it will be your fault. You may get off for kidnapping, but you will never get off for murder."

He stopped, pulled down his sleeves, and stood at attention. "Now you pay attention bitch. If you say anything, and I mean anything, at the hospital then you are correct, I will be a murderer. It will be the end of you and that baby. Do you understand?"

"I swear that I won't say a word. Let's go right now to the Emergency Room at the Kings Hospital."

Astrid wrapped Anja in a soft blanket and rushed to the door, waiting for Aksel to unlock it. Before he opened the door, he handcuffed her wrist to his. It was uncomfortable to maneuver, but they got into the van.

"Listen to me," he said threateningly. "We are a husband and wife and our baby fell off the bed. If you try any tricks, I will burn down your parents' house."

Aksel drove as slowly as he could to aggravate Astrid. They crawled over the bridge toward the closest hospital, the Kings Hospital. As they approached the entrance and Astrid was beginning to feel relief, Aksel accelerated and drove right past.

"Stop!" she said, "Where are you going?"

"To the other one in Erdem. We can't go here, someone may recognize us."

Aksel then accelerated, driving fast and erratically, speeding through red traffic lights. Astrid could feel Anja's regulated breathing, so she became less frantic. Anja also had her eyes open, focusing on her mother's face. This was a good sign.

They arrived at the hospital, and Aksel stopped in the parking lot. He grabbed Astrid's wrist and unlocked the handcuff. He held tightly onto her jacket as they walked into the emergency entrance. Astrid went directly to a nurse at the front desk and explained that the baby had fallen. She immediately ushered them into a small office where another woman in hospital scrubs told them to sit down.

'Why are you here?" she asked.

"Our baby daughter fell off the bed," said Astrid. The lady asked the baby's name and date of birth. She typed the information into a computer. "Can I have your ID?" she asked.

"I left it at home," said Astrid.

"Your ID?" she said to Aksel.

"In our rush, we left everything behind."

They were immediately led to an examination cubicle. It was a bare room, with a hospital bed and two chairs. Medical equipment lined the green walls. They sat in silence. Anja had fallen asleep in her mother's arms. Aksel stood up and paced the small enclosure, mumbling to himself.

A tall, blonde woman in a white coat with a stethoscope around her neck walked in and introduced herself as the doctor. Her assistant was behind her.

"Please explain what happened," she said to Astrid.

"The baby was on the bed, and I was about to change her clothes, when I turned around to get something. In one second, she rolled off the bed onto the floor."

"Uh-huh," said the doctor, nodding her head.

Astrid could tell that she didn't believe the story.

"Please put the baby on the bed," she instructed.

Astrid lay a sleeping Anja on the bed. The doctor started examining her, feeling her arms, legs, and body, then lifting her up and checking her head. She opened each of Anja's eyes and looked at them with a bright light. She listened to her heartbeat with the stethoscope. She ran her hands up and down her spine. The doctor looked at the bruise on the side of her forehead.

"Are you the baby's mother?" she asked Astrid, looking at her intensely.

"Yes," Astrid replied.

"Are you the father?" the doctor asked Aksel.

"Yes," he said.

"By law, I have to ask you this question," said the doctor. "Did either of you hit the baby?"

"Of course not," said Aksel, offended.

"Drop her?"

They both shook their heads.

"Shake her?"

"What is this?" asked Aksel, annoyed. "You don't think that we had anything to do with this?"

Astrid suddenly spoke out loud. "Excuse me," she said. "I can smell that my baby has a dirty diaper. Can I please change her?"

"In a minute," said the doctor. "I need to finish examining her."

Astrid paid no attention.

"She smells really bad," she said, bending down and putting her nose in Anja's diaper. "Yes, it's a big runny one," she said. "I can see poop coming out of the sides."

As she pulled Anja's pajama pants off and was about to open the Velcro strips on the diaper, Aksel started retching. He pinched his nose shut and started making loud guttural sounds.

"Just go out of the room for one second," Astrid said to him. "Step into the corridor."

The doctor and her assistant looked at Astrid, annoyed.

"We can first finish the examination and then you can change her," said the assistant.

Aksel was walking in circles with his hands cupped over his mouth, heaving loudly.

"I said go out until I finish changing her," Astrid commanded. Then she turned to the doctor. "My husband gets very queasy about bodily functions," she explained.

Aksel raced out of the room, and they could hear him throwing up in the corridor.

Astrid whispered urgently to the doctor, "Please help. We are kidnapped. Call the police. Now!"

The women both looked up with big eyes and open mouths, shocked. The assistant left the room.

Aksel poked his head through the door. "Are you finished?" he asked, blowing his nose and wiping his mouth with tissues. Someone had given him a bottle of water and calmed him down.

"Yes," said Astrid. "All clear. It's all been cleaned."

The doctor then proceeded to ask routine questions. She examined Anja all over again. She again held a light to her eyes and had her follow the beam. She pressed and prodded her body.

"Is she OK?" Asrid asked.

"She looks fine, but we will have to do a brain scan. It seems that she hit her head."

"How long will that take?" asked Aksel. "We are in a hurry to beat the traffic."

"Not too long. We are waiting for the pediatric radiology department to come and get you."

"Such a fuss about nothing," grumbled Aksel.

The examining room door opened and three officers with guns drawn rushed into the room. They grabbed Aksel and handcuffed his hands behind his back.

"What are you doing?" he said as his face went white. He realized that he had been tricked. He looked at Astrid with pure hate. "You will be sorry," he said.

They led him away shouting, "This is a mistake. I have done nothing wrong."

Astrid collapsed on the bed with Anja in her arms. The doctor put her arms around her. Astrid could not stop shaking. A nurse covered her with a warm blanket.

"You are safe now," she said. "We will protect you."

A team of hospital personnel crowded into the room. No one said a word—there was a shocked silence.

"I am Astrid Larsen, and this is my baby Anja Larsen. We have both been kept against our will."

"We have all been looking for you for a long time," someone said. "You were so smart the way you maneuvered this."

"We know all about you and your daughter. The whole country has been praying for your safe return," said a man in a suit.

"I want to call my husband and my parents," Astrid said in a hollow voice. She felt as though every ounce of her body was numb. The only thing that mattered was that her baby was safe.

A woman in a security uniform had found Astrid's parent's phone number in their database. She dialed the number and a woman picked up.

"Hello, this is the Copenhagen Security Police Division. Is this Astrid Larsen's mother?"

"Yes."

"I have very good news for you." She handed the phone to Astrid.

"Hello Mother," Astrid said softly. "I am safe, and Anja is safe. We are at the hospital in Erdem. Can you come and get us? I want to come home."

CHAPTER THIRTY

SARDINIA

Adela was not happy when her mother told her that Signor Rossi and she were getting married.

"Mama, please, you are too old for that," she said.

"I'm not too old to want companionship in my last years," Signora Melis said. "I deserve some happiness in my life."

"You are happy just being who you are, a mother and grandmother. What else do you need?" Adela folded her arms and pouted. She was offended that her mother would even consider remarriage. "How can you besmirch Papa's name? It is a disgrace," she added.

"Papa has been gone a long time. You have your own life now, Adela. I need a life, too."

"Our life is your life. Look at Signora Garibaldi and Signora Petrucci, they are widows and are happy as they are. Why are you looking for happiness? It's not right at your age."

"I am not asking for your permission," said Signora Melis firmly. "I am telling you that we are getting married."

"Why him?" said Adela. "He is not your type. You have nothing in common."

"I'm not debating this with you," said Signora Melis. "I just hope you will accept the situation and be happy for us."

Adela stormed off and Signora Melis could hear her complaining to Luca. Signor Rossi came in from watering the garden.

"I told Adela our good news," Signora Melis said.

"What did she say?" he asked while washing his hands in the kitchen sink.

"She is a little taken aback but she will come around," said Signora Melis.

Luca came to the table with Mira, but Adela remained in her room saying that she wasn't hungry. They were going to move to an apartment of their own before too long, and Signora Melis felt that was a good thing for them all. She had become attached to her little granddaughter. Mira was now walking and was a happy, mischievous child. Her big blue eyes and heart-shaped mouth gave her an air of sweet innocence, but she had a mind of her own. She knew what she liked and what she didn't and would let one know. Signora Melis thought that was a good thing; no one would step over this child.

"I hear that congratulations are in order," Luca said to Signora Melis and Signor Rossi.

"Thank you," said Signor Rossi. He poured wine into each of their glasses. "Let's make a toast," he said, raising his glass.

"To health and happiness," responded Luca.

The three of them clinked glasses.

"When is the wedding?" asked Luca.

"Exactly a week from today," said Signora Melis. "Just the family and a few friends will join us in the church. Mama Sophia will be roasting a pig at the trattoria for the occasion."

Mira toddled off toward the door and fell, knocking her head on the edge of the coffee table. She let out a big cry, which brought Adela running out of the bedroom.

"Oh, my darling," she said, picking her up and rubbing the red mark on her forehead. "See, in one minute you have already forgotten about your granddaughter. You are so taken with this man that you can't think of anything else!"

"Don't be ridiculous," said Signora Melis.

"Luca, didn't I tell you that my mother has changed? She is not the mother that I knew since she met Signor Rossi."

"Adela," interjected Signor Rossi. "Your mother will always be your mother. Nothing will change that. I will never take the place of your father. Let's just all get along and be there for each other."

The following week, the wedding went smoothly without a hitch. On Signora Melis's side came her two best friends, and her aunt and cousins from Cagliari. She wore a simple cream dress that covered her knees. She had pinned a white gardenia in her hair. Adela and Mira wore matching pale pink organza dresses.

Signor Rossi wore a brown suit with an unbuttoned shirt and a white carnation on his lapel. He had no family present, but the entire bocce team came to wish him well. The blessing was given by the Padre, followed by a short sermon that Signor Rossie and Signora Melis's union was ordained and blessed by the Lord who had a hand in putting them together. At the end of the service, the Padre told Signor Rossie that he could kiss his bride. He bent over and kissed her lightly on the lips. She blushed and someone giggled. Adela rolled her eyes and jabbed her husband in the ribs.

The wedding party and guests walked the four blocks to Mama Sophia's Trattoria. It was a warm but windy day. The ladies had to hold down their dresses to keep them from blowing upward. Dry leaves swirled around their ankles as they teetered on their low heels along the uneven paving. Mama Sophia had opened the back terrace especially for the occasion. The high stone walls protected the area from the wind. The white clothed tables were shaded by white umbrellas, and the settings looked festive with sunflowers in glass vases.

Mama Sophia's main cook was Alberto, an ancient man who had worked his way up from dishwasher to cook over the thirty years he had worked in the kitchen. Alberto was a sinewy figure, with a hump on his back from bending over a stove and continuously stirring hot bubbling polenta and stews. He was never seen without a lit cigarette in his mouth, even while cooking. No one dared cross him because there were rumors that he was the connection the "bosses" called when they needed a favor to quiet someone—forever. Some said he started the rumor on his own, but no one dared to challenge his reputation.

His *su porceddu*, suckling pig roasting slowly on a spit over the embers for many hours, was renowned throughout the island. After the cooking was done, he flavored the "fall off the bone" meat with myrtle and rosemary, and the diners all agreed that they had never eaten such a tasty dish. Alberto had started grilling the suckling pig the evening before the wedding feast. By the time the guests arrived, the pig was displayed on a large metal platter, ready to be carved.

It was a festive meal with a lot of wine and good feelings. Three men with lyrical tenor voices were hired to sing folk songs acapella. The men sang hauntingly, using their throats as an instrument, their voices raising and lowering while telling a story of love and its rewards.

By the time the *Gato de mendula*—a crunchy cake with toasted almonds and orange— was served, the bride was feeling squeamish. A hot flush crept up her body to her head. Beads of perspiration formed on her upper lip, while cramping spasms gripped her stomach. She bent over, breathing heavily.

"*Amore*, is something wrong?" asked her concerned new husband.

"I'm not feeling very well," she said, clutching her stomach.

He passed her a glass of water. "Have a sip," he said. "It will make you feel better."

She took a sip but then heaved, spewing green vomit all over herself and Signor Rossi.

"Oh, my dear," he said, jumping up. "Quick, someone bring some cloths."

He immediately wiped Signora Melis's face, but the waves of nausea kept erupting as she threw up and cried at the same time. The guests were all upset. They tried to figure out how to help, but the more they tried to comfort her, the sicker she got.

Mama Sophia limped her way as fast as she could to Signora Melis's side.

"You poor thing," she said. "Signor Rossi, help me carry her inside."

He lifted Signora Melis under her arms and Mama Sophia lifted her legs and they carried her like two drunken sailors into the cool air of the restaurant and laid her on the cold floor. With strength that she didn't know she had, Signora Melis jumped up and raced into the bathroom. She just made it before the avalanche of roasted pig remains filled up the toilet bowl.

Signor Rossi held her up while liquid came out from both ends. He called for someone to call the doctor. Dottore

Bertollini came running with his bag. He was on call twenty-four hours every day. He knew Signora Melis well, just as he knew everyone in the town since he had treated most of the townsfolk at some time or another. Dr. Bertollini had done and seen it all, medically. What he hadn't learned in medical school fifty years before he had learned from experience. He walked into the restaurant, briefly looked at Signora Melis, and told her she had food poisoning.

"Not from my food," said Mama Sophia, aghast.

"Yes, from your food," the doctor stated.

"In all the years I have had this restaurant, no one has ever gotten sick," she said.

"There is always a first time, and this is it," the doctor said, listening to Signora Melis's heart with his stethoscope. He opened his bag, took out a syringe, and gave her a shot on her behind.

When she felt better, Signor Rossi and Luca dragged her home.

"What a way to end my wedding," she cried bitterly. "What a terrible way to start our marriage," she sobbed.

"Dearest, this is a good way to start the marriage. Things can only improve from here," said Signor Rossi. "And now you have me to take care of you."

That night, many of the wedding guests got sick. Dr. Bertollini was a very busy man, running from house to house.

The wedding guests whispered that perhaps Alberto had slaughtered the pig too soon and kept it in the sun too long without refrigeration.

No one received any explanations, but a few days later, in the early morning when Signor Rossi went to start his car, he saw that someone had scraped long lines all around the body of the vehicle. He knew who it was—the bent-over cook at Mama Sophia's.

* * *

Adela felt happy and serene in her new apartment. She felt a sense of relief moving from her mother's house to their own place. As much as she loved her mother, she knew it was time for her little family to be independent and have a place of their own.

The three-story building was just two blocks away from her mother's house, yet it felt like a town away. Signora Melis could visit whenever she wanted, and she did, and Adela would go to her mother's house to chat and have coffee and a meal.

Signora Melis still made the time to babysit Mira anytime Adela needed to be somewhere else. She relished those times with her granddaughter, who had now started putting words together. Nothing had changed for her since she married Signor Rossi, yet everything had changed, for the better. He of course was now living in the main house and sharing her double bed. Their pre-marriage daily routine remained the same—Signor Rossi doing his chores and Signora Melis busy with her daily tasks, but with a feeling of warmth and security.

Luca had been given a promotion at the trucking company; he was now a manager of the entire Italy/ Scandinavia territory. He continued to truck goods to Denmark which was his favorite route.

One morning at breakfast he asked Adela, "How would you and Mira like to come with me on one of my trips to Copenhagen?"

"Don't you think the long drive will be too much for Mira?" she asked while pouring coffee into their cups from the silver Moka pot.

"It's about a thirty-hour drive, but we can break it up. One night in Rome and another in Germany. I will book the hotels; it will be fun."

Instead of feeling excited, Adela felt apprehensive. The first thing that crossed her mind was Luca's clandestine trips with Pia. She didn't want to follow the same route and stir up sad memories.

"What is bothering you?" Luca asked. He knew his wife's moods well.

"Nothing," she said. "Maybe we will come with you when you take another route. Copenhagen is very far, over two thousand kilometers."

Luca got up from the table and approached his wife. "If you are concerned about my fling with Pia, do not worry about that," he reassured her. "It was something I deeply regret, but it resulted in having Mira, which I will never regret."

"It will take me time to build up trust for you again," she said.

"I know, I will do everything in my power for you to gain my trust again."

"Will Mira be comfortable for so many hours on the road?"

"I have a new, bigger, better truck with a lot more space. It will be like a little vacation."

Although Adela felt eager to go on a little adventure, she was apprehensive. Her life revolved around her town and the close perimeters. The only time she had ever left Sardinia was on a school trip to Rome. She had been overwhelmed by the architecture, the crowds, the traffic, and the vast size of the town, but she never forgot the thrill of it all. Adela told Luca that she would agree to go with him with the condition that he promised to stop for toilet breaks and food whenever she wanted to.

"Of course, *amore*," he said. "We will also go on a ferry with the truck, but we can get out at any time to walk around." He knew that she didn't like to feel trapped.

Their rental apartment was small but modern. It was newly built. The most exciting feature was a brand-new washer and dryer. Adela couldn't get over the convenience of having her clothes washed at the press of a button, then dried in an hour.She wished that her mother could adapt to the modern ways and not make more work for herself. But Adela conceded that her mother was a creature of habit and enjoyed the ritual of washing and hanging the laundry by hand.

Before the trip to Copenhagen, Adela had a dental appointment, so she dropped Mira off at her mother's house.

She immediately noticed that her mother looked different. Always a pretty woman, she now glowed, and a sparkle had returned to her eyes. She even looked younger, and she had shed her matronly clothes and opted for form-fitting stylish dresses. Signora Melis now wore her hair longer, tying it back in a loose chignon.

"Love suits you, Mama," Adela said. She felt happy to see her mother happy.

"Thank you, my sweet girl. I believe that I not only found the right man, but I found myself."

Signora Melis picked Mira up and danced with her around the room. "This is my pride and joy," she said, hugging her. Mira squealed with delight; she adored her grandmother.

As Adela reached the corner to turn into the street where the dental office was, she spotted Pia coming out of the hair salon. Instinctively, she wanted to turn around and head in the opposite direction, but instead she held her head high and went to greet her nemesis.

"*Ciao,*" Adela said. "I thought you had left for Bari."

"We are leaving next week. I am just finishing up with my clients." Pia stood awkwardly. Not knowing where to put her hands, she placed them in her skirt pockets and twirled from side to side.

"Pia, I wish you good luck and I wish you happiness. Even after everything we went through, I want the best for you."

"*Grazie,*" she said.

"The only thing I can't understand is how you ended up with Alessandro. Despite knowing all his faults, you are going to marry him."

"I know, I also question myself," she said faltering. "The only reason I think is that no man has ever paid attention to me or wanted me. They have always used me for one thing—sex. I have such low self-esteem and I don't feel that I deserve better. Alessandro—a good looking womanizer who can get almost any woman that he chooses—paid me attention and asked me to marry him."

"It sounds like you need to talk to a therapist. You don't have to settle for someone who you know is not right for you."

"I believe him when he tells me that he wants to marry a local girl and start a family, and that I am his best prospect."

"What about love?" asked Adela. "Do you love him? Does he love you?"

"I don't think there is that kind of love. It's more of a convenience for both of us," she said.

"I have to run—I have a dentist appointment. I wish you the best of luck and hope it works out for you," said Adela.

"Just one more thing," said Pia. "I am so happy that Mira has such a wonderful mother and father. That brings me peace. I hope that in time you will keep in touch and let me know how she is doing."

They both waved and went their separate ways.

The day they left for Copenhagen it was raining. The truck had been loaded with pallets of wine the night before.

It was too large to park close to their home, so Adela and Luca walked in the rain back and forth under a big umbrella carrying their supplies to load in the truck. Signora Melis had prepared meals for the road, packed in glass-covered casserole dishes. She did not believe in plastic.

"Plastic has toxins," she said, "that permeate the food and cause cancer."

When she had a strong opinion on something there was no way of changing her mind. The glass containers had to be washed and dried before returning them to their owner, but Adela agreed that it was a small price to pay for the delicious meals.

After the front cab had been packed up, Adela carried Mira to the truck and put her in the baby seat. Luca helped them climb up the ledge into the front seat. They blew kisses to Signora Melis and Signor Rossi and they were on their way.

Once they hit the autostrada, Luca picked up speed. Adela found it curiously satisfying to be so high off the ground. Looking down at the traffic gave her a sense of advantage. She liked the way the cars moved out of the way as their truck approached.

"I feel like the queen in her castle," she said to Luca.

"It's a good feeling," said Luca. "But it's not easy to drive. I have to be very cautious and alert at all times."

Luca pulled up to take the first ferry ride over to Italy. They remained in the truck throughout the crossing. Adela placed her mother's food on a blanket, and they had a picnic lunch at the back of the truck. Mira, taken with the excitement and novelty of the event, squealed with excitement.

Back on the road, Adela saw her husband through different eyes. She had not realized how competent and capable he was at his job. She reached out to put her hand on his leg. He turned and smiled. It was the first time in a long time that Adela had shown him any affection.

Green pastures, dotted with spring flowers, flashed through the windows. Hilltop villages with ancient dwellings were precariously balancing like Jenga blocks about to topple over. It was impossible to imagine how they had remained that way for hundreds of years.

Close to Rome, Luca turned off the highway and stopped in a town where he could park the truck. They walked around the block to a small hotel with a restaurant. On the outside the building was dilapidated, needing a fresh coat of paint, but inside, the bare bones were clean and fresh. A grumpy unshaven man, sucking a toothpick, showed them to their room. There was a single bed made up and a crib for Mira. Luca asked if they could have a room with a double bed.

"Just squeeze together," he said. "It will be good for your marriage."

The dining room with three tables and no other guests was dismal. There was no choice of food. A woman came out, possibly the innkeeper's wife, looking more depressed than her husband. When Mira, instinctively feeling her gloom, waved at her, she merely sighed and turned her head. The menu of the day was Osso Buco, veal shanks in a thick tomato-based sauce. The only side it came with was fresh sourdough bread. It could have been that Adela and Luca were so hungry that the meal tasted so good, but they both agreed that it was the best Osso Buco that they had ever tasted.

When the lady came to clear the plates, Luca told her that. She never smiled, but she pinched Mira's cheeks so hard that she cried.

The young family left early the next morning and headed for Germany. Now that there were automatic weigh stations, it made trucking so much easier for Luca. By using sensors embedded in the road surfaces, combined with cameras recognizing license plates, the truck could be weighed without having to stop.

"We will sleep in Puttgarden, then the next morning we will take the ferry over to Rodby," said Luca. "It's about forty-five minutes and we stay in the truck."

"Where are we going to sleep?" asked Adela. "I am exhausted from sitting and doing nothing," she laughed. "Are you?"

"I am used to this," he said. "I am not tired. We will be staying overnight at Gasthaus Die Schone. It's not bad, I've stayed there before."

"With Pia?"

"No. No. You have to stop worrying about that," Luca said to Adela.

When they arrived at the Guest House, Luca found it difficult to park the truck.

A gardener who was trimming the bushes outside the Gasthaus told Luca with hand signs that there was a parking lot on the next street.

He had a big, beaming smile and with a lot of head nodding and pointing, he directed Luca to the parking lot.

Adela and Mira had already checked into their room, a comfortable chalet with wooden walls and wooden beams. Unlike the place in Italy, this had a large wooden bed with a cozy white duvet. They had already eaten, so Adela and Mira snuggled up in the warm bed and soon fell asleep. Luca spent some time on his phone mapping out the last leg of the trip to Copenhagen.

In the morning, after a hearty breakfast of a farmer's omelet—made with ham, bacon, potatoes, and onion—the family was ready to go on their way.

When Luca opened the door of the cab, he immediately saw that everything was in disarray. He was a meticulously neat person, and everything in his truck had a place.

"Someone has been in the truck," he said in disbelief.

"Why do you say that?" asked Adela, peering inside.

She saw what he meant. The glove compartment was open, and all the travel documents and papers were strewn on the floor. Their duffle bags, packed with clothes and items for the trip, were missing, as well as their sleeping bags, camera, and the toolbox for the truck. Everything that could be lifted was gone.

"Who could have stolen all our things?" said Luca in shock.

Adela burst out crying but quickly stopped herself so that Mira wouldn't become upset.

"The gardener!" exclaimed Adela. "He was the only one who knew where we had parked."

"He didn't have a key; how did he break in?" said Luca.

They raced back to the guesthouse and found the owner sweeping the entrance floor. Luca told him what had happened. They both could understand English.

"It's the gardener," said Luca. "He helped me park the truck."

"What gardener?" said the hotel proprietor.

"The small, plump man with a round face. He was trimming your bushes."

"We don't have a gardener," said the proprietor. "I do all my own gardening."

"Do you know who I am talking about?" said Luca.

"No. I have never seen or heard about this person."

"Should we make a police report?" said Adela to her husband.

"There is no point," said Luca. "We are in a hurry, we are nonresidents, and it will be impossible to prove."

Dejected, they climbed into the truck and headed for Denmark.

"It could have been worse," said Luca. "No one got hurt and it's only material things. They can always be replaced."

CHAPTER THIRTY-ONE

COPENHAGEN

"We interrupt this regular broadcast with breaking news. A person of interest has been arrested in the case of the missing baby and her mother, Astrid Larsen. Both mother and child have been found safe and in good health.

"There will be a news conference broadcast this evening on this station at 7:00 p.m. from outside the Danish Police Headquarters.

"We now take you back to the program in progress."

Astrid was sitting on the sofa with her mother and father watching the TV monitor. She had a blanket wrapped around her shoulders and was drinking hot tea.

Gudrun squeezed her daughter's hand. She wanted to hug her and never let her go. She had held Anja since they had come home and hadn't put her down.

They looked at the photo of the kidnapper's mugshot on the screen. Aksel looked deranged, his hair messy and his eyes wild. They had not asked Astrid the details of her imprisonment. They were advised by a psychologist not to pry for details. She would tell them when she is ready.

Jens kept looking over at his daughter with tears in his eyes. He could not fathom the suffering that she had gone through, and he felt guilty that he had not been able to protect his daughter. He agonized that he didn't hire a security guard for her after Anja had been kidnapped, but they had never imagined that Astrid would be a target as well.

Anton was ecstatic that his wife and daughter had returned home safely. He had not been a religious man, but he had prayed so many times for their safe return, and now that his prayers had been answered, he found purpose and confirmation of his faith.

The most difficult situation to resolve was the navigation of their relationship with their closest friends and neighbors.

It was their son who was the monster in this story. As soon as Astrid and Anja arrived home, Dr Sorensen called.

"We are devastated about our son," he said to Jens. "We don't know what to say or what to do. We can't believe what he did. We want you to know how ashamed we are that we raised a person who could do this." Dr. Sorensen, overcome by emotion, had to hand the phone to his wife.

"We are so relieved that Astrid and Anja are safe. We will never get over the guilt of our son causing so much suffering," she said.

They were on speaker phone. Gudrun spoke next. "We don't blame you for what Aksel did," she said. "We know that you had nothing to do with this."

"We are broken," continued Dr. Sorensen. "We raised a stranger."

Clara added, "We will always love our son, but we hate what he did to you. If he goes to jail for the rest of his life, we agree that he deserves it."

There were no more words to say. After the phone call, they sat silently and still as the sky darkened, throwing shadows in the unlit room, moving only when Anja called out for her mother. They felt peace at last.

* * *

Mira was bouncing up and down on the hotel bed. The higher she jumped, the louder she laughed.

"Stop that, silly," said Adela. "Soon you will fall off the bed and bump your head."

"Oh my God!" said Luca. He was looking at the TV screen. He jumped up and turned up the volume.

Adela spun around and knew exactly what he was watching. There was a headshot of a man on the screen and an announcement that a person of interest had been found in the kidnapping of the Danish mother and her daughter.

"First he took the baby, then her mother. It's a miracle that they found them safe."

"Is this the baby that you built up our whole story about?" asked Adela, startled.

"Yes. I was here when the news story broke about a baby girl who had gone missing. That was when I concocted the story of how I found Mira."

"Why did you first lead me to believe that she was abandoned?"

"I stupidly thought that I would tell you that I found her, and then make you suspicious that she was the kidnapped child. I tried to make it convincing. But it backfired."

"Can you believe that we are in Copenhagen right at the time when they caught him," she said. "I feel so relieved that they are all safe."

"This hotel is close to the headquarters where the news conference will be tonight. We should go and watch," said Luca.

"Do you think so?"

"Yes. It would give us closure. What were the chances of being in this city at the same time? After dinner we can take a walk and head over there."

Adela was intrigued by how each country had an entirely different atmosphere and feeling. Denmark was a marked contrast to Italy. The smells were different, the food was different—one wasn't better than the other, just different. The first thing Adela noticed was how differently the Danish people carried themselves. They walked straighter, prouder, their Viking heritage shining through, whereas the Italians walked slower, looking around, observing their surroundings. The Danes kept their hands still when conversing, while the Italians couldn't talk without using their hands. Every person she observed around her in Copenhagen looked intelligent, worldly, bookish. She mentioned this to Luca.

"You can't really tell much about people in such a short time," he said. "Often people put on a façade, and it takes time to get to know the real person."

"I agree," said Adela, "but I'm observing first impressions."

Luca was aware that on his visits to Denmark he noticed that his sense of humor did not align with theirs. What he perceived as funny, they didn't. He recalled telling some lighthearted jokes to his Danish colleagues, and they stared at him blankly. He soon learned not to engage in that manner.

Adela also noticed the love of children that both cultures enjoyed. Families playing in the park, the children pink cheeked, running around having fun. The whole town of Copenhagen was geared toward children. There were playgrounds, children's museums, and bookstores all over the city. Children were welcome everywhere. Everyone rode bicycles, including mothers with front carts that carried their small children out and about. It was their main mode of transportation, unlike the Italians, who did not encourage riding a bicycle in case their child fell off and got hurt. The Danes were much more relaxed with their children's safety, urging them to be unafraid of the world. Italians would be deemed overprotective, fueling fear of unknown dangers. Adela wanted to learn about different cultures and take the good to incorporate into her life.

"This is why it is important to travel," she said to Luca. They were sitting at an outdoor café drinking coffee.

"Even the coffee is different," he laughed.

"Which do you prefer?" she asked.

"Italian, of course. When it comes to food and coffee, no one beats Italy," he said. "Travel is the best education," he concurred, wiping Mira's sticky fingers after she ate a pastry.

"We should do it more often," Adela said. "I would really like to visit France someday."

"Why France?"

"Paris. I've always wanted to visit Paris. It sounds so romantic."

"That sounds like a good idea," Luca said. He leaned forward to hold her hand. He was feeling more positive about their relationship; it felt like he was dating his wife all over again.

They went back to the hotel and all three of them took a nap. The ringing of Adela's phone woke them.

"*Ciao*, Mama," Adela said. "I was napping but I'm up now. How are you? We are all fine; we are in

Copenhagen. The trip went smoothly. Luca unloaded the wine at the warehouse, and we are staying for a few days in a hotel."

As Luca walked into the room from taking a shower, Adela mouthed, "It's my mother," to him.

"Sad news?" said Adela, sitting up straight. "What sad news?"

Luca moved closer to Adela to listen to what her mother was saying about "sad news."

"A car accident?" Adela went white. "On the highway? They crashed into the mountainside?"

"Who? Who?" asked Luca.

Adela turned to him. "Pia and Alessandro, they crashed on the way to Bari."

They both froze.

"*Dio mio*!" said Luca.

"They both are dead?" said Adela. "That can't be true, Mama. Are you sure?"

She leaned her head on Luca's chest and cried. "Mama, I'll be OK. Don't worry about me. I'll be OK."

She turned off the phone and lay in Luca's arms. She was trembling from shock.

"What happened?" said Luca.

"They were driving in the Ferrari to Bari. Alessandro was racing, he lost control. and they smashed into the mountain side. I didn't like what she did to me, but I still loved her," cried Adela.

Mira crawled over her father on the bed toward her mother and laid her head on her shoulder as if she understood that she was sad.

"Do you still want to go to the press conference?" Luca asked after they ate and felt a bit better.

"We should go. I will be alright. I want to see that this terrible man gets what he deserves," Adela said.

They left the hotel with Mira in a stroller and walked the short block to the Copenhagen Police Headquarters. As they got closer, they could see bright spotlights illuminating the entrance to the main door with a podium set up and a microphone. TV cameras and crew lined up in front of the podium at the bottom of the steps. Journalists from local and international newspapers and media sources stood in the front rows. Crowds had gathered, and by the time Luca and Adela arrived, it was difficult to find a place up front.

Luca jostled their way to get a better view. At exactly 7 p.m., three uniformed police officers exited the door. Then Anton and Astrid, led by a female officer, joined the line. Adela noted how vulnerable and frail the baby's parents looked. They stood with blank expressions, blinded by the bright lights.

The senior officer spoke first.

"Good evening. I am Officer Peter Hansen from the Danish Ministry of Justice. On my left are Officer Lars Borgen and Officer Michael Jensen, and on my right are Anna Anderson and Mr. and Mrs. Larsen.

"On Monday morning, we apprehended a person of interest in the kidnapping of Astrid Larsen and her daughter Anja Larsen. Our police force was notified by the Erdem Hospital of suspicious behavior of a man who was with the victims. Thank you to them for their observant and quick response. The person apprehended allegedly as the kidnapper of the mother and the baby is the thirty-nine-year-old male, Aksel Sebastain Sorensen of Copenhagen. As events unfold, we will be keeping you updated. In the meantime, we ask you to please allow the Sorensen family to heal in peace. Thank you very much."

The journalists in the crowd shouted out questions.

"Where were the victims kept?"

Officer Lars Borgen approached the podium and spoke into the microphone.

"We cannot say. This is still under investigation."

"Did the perpetrator know the victims?"

"We cannot say. This is an ongoing investigation."

"Why did he take the baby first and then kidnap her mother?"

"As I said, this is not up for discussion at this time. As events unfold, we will keep you all informed." The officer collected his papers and left the podium.

Officer Jensen closed the conference and led everyone off the dais.

"I feel so sorry for those parents," said Adela. "They look so traumatized."

Luca and Adela sat on a bench close to the building. There was a small garden where Mira was playing. She picked little yellow flowers from a bush and brought them to her mother. Back and forth she went.

Adela, with the flowers that Mira picked tucked behind her ears, turned to Luca. "I have deep feelings of guilt that I took a baby without knowing her background."

Luca answered, "I led you to believe that the baby was abandoned."

"I believed it because I wanted to believe it. The truth is that I never questioned anything. I didn't want to know the details. I think about that a lot. Who am I to judge anyone else?"

Just then they heard voices and the police officers from the news conference walked out the side door of the building. The full moon illuminated their faces and Adela watched as they left. Mira was still picking flowers outside the side door. The door swung open, and Astrid and her husband walked down the stairs. Astrid came down first and Adela was surprised how tall she was. Mira was happily chatting in baby talk when Astrid stopped in her tracks. She bent down and tousled Mira's blonde curls. Mira smiled at her and gave her a flower.

Astrid turned and faced Adela. "She is so cute," she said, locking eyes. As she walked away, she called out, "She reminds me so much of my daughter."

ABOUT THE AUTHOR

Bonita Fabian was born in South Africa and spent most of her life traveling and writing stories about her experiences for magazines and newspapers. She lived in Italy for a few years where she fell in love with the people and the culture. After her four children were raised, she realized her lifelong aspiration of becoming an accomplished novelist. She lives with her husband in Miami, Florida.

Made in the USA
Las Vegas, NV
09 April 2024

88461848R00166